More praise for James Melville and THE BODY WORE BROCADE

"Meville once again provides some unexpected twists in a beautifully crafted novel full of insight into the Japanese character, personified in Superintendent Otani, who can proudly take a place among the greatest of fictional detectives."
—*The Midwest Book Review*

"Intriguing and witty . . . An interesting and insightful portrait of Japan in our time."
—*The Naperville Sun*

"The plot, a beautifully textured one, interweaves the relationships and character of those involved, and is finally worked out while giving the reader satisfying insights into the complexities of human nature."
—*Rocky Mount Telegram*

"An intriguing excursion into the minds, lives and culture of a re-emergent world power."
—*Prime Suspects*

THE BODY
WORE
BROCADE

James Melville

FAWCETT CREST • NEW YORK

A Fawcett Crest Book
Published by Ballantine Books
Copyright © 1992 by James Melville

Library of Congress Catalog Card Number: 92-17868

ISBN 0-449-22189-X

This edition published by arrangement with Charles Scribner's Sons, an imprint of Macmillan Publishing Company.

Manufactured in the United States of America

First Ballantine Books Edition: May 1994

10 9 8 7 6 5 4 3 2 1

PRINCIPAL CHARACTERS IN THE STORY

Law and Order
Superintendent Tetsuo Otani, Hyogo prefectural police
Hanae, his wife
Professor Michiko Yanagida, Hanae's younger sister
Inspector Takeshi Hara, Michiko's lover
Inspector Jiro Kimura
Inspector Hachiro (Ninja) Noguchi
Woman Senior Detective Junko Migishima
Patrolman Ken'ichi Migishima, her husband
Assistant Inspector Chiba
District Prosecutor Akamatsu

Others
Hideki Suminoe, wealthy amateur of Noh
Koichi Suminoe, his elder nephew
Toshio Suminoe, his younger nephew
Dr. Yoshiko Suminoe, Hideki's sister
Yasuo Iida, Hideki's driver/handyman
Emiko Iida, Yasuo's wife and Hideki's housekeeper
Susumu Narita, Hideki's legal adviser

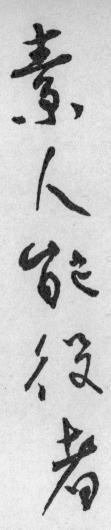

素人能役者

The Japanese version of the title reads *Shiroto Noh Yakusha*, or "The Amateur of Noh," and the calligraphy is by Mie Kimata.

FOREWORD

FORMER SUPERINTENDENT TETSUO OTANI NOW LIVES IN RE-
tirement with his wife Hanae on the island of Awaji in the
Inland Sea not far from Kobe, in order that they may see
a good deal of their daughter Akiko, her husband Akira
Shimizu, and their grandson Kazuo. Mr. Otani is no longer
involved with criminal investigation work. At least, this is
what he claims; and he turns the question when asked to
confirm or deny suggestions that his frequent visits to
Tokyo and occasional trips overseas are necessitated by his
new status as a special consultant to the National Police
Agency of Japan.

He is quietly amused—and, I suspect, rather flat-
tered—by the knowledge that many of the cases in which
he was involved during his long and distinguished official
career have been recorded in semi-fictional form and published in Britain, the United States, Germany, Italy and
other countries, as well as in Japan itself. Often during our
occasional meetings he has chided me with tolerant good
humour about my inadequacies as an observer of and com-
mentator on things Japanese. All the same, he keeps a full
set of the Otani books in his house, and Mrs. Otani unobtrusively draws them to the attention of visitors.

Mr. Otani readily agreed to my original request that he
should allow me to interview him at length over a period of
several days following his retirement last year; but it took
a lot of persuasion to convince him that, in place of a so-
called "in-depth" magazine interview, his admirers outside
Japan would appreciate much more an account in his own
words of his last investigation. He is a modest man, and
like most Japanese is normally reticent to a degree about

his private life. Once he grew accustomed to the ever-present tape-recorder, however, he revealed himself as no mean raconteur, and was much more forthcoming than I had dared to hope he might be.

In offering to act as his amanuensis I pointed out that I would be reporting his words to readers the majority of whom would be unlikely to have first-hand knowledge of Japan. With characteristic sensitivity he went to considerable pains to explain the background to the extent that he thought necessary; and always responded to my occasional requests for further enlightenment. The narrative is presented as if its author is still in police service, and when it was recorded that was technically true, since at the time he was enjoying a few weeks of accumulated leave on full pay pending his formal retirement from the service.

Mr. Otani insists that he doesn't understand a word of English, and when I submitted my draft to him he passed it to his friend and former colleague Inspector (now Superintendent) Jiro Kimura to read and approve on his behalf. Superintendent Kimura was enthusiastic and probably much too uncritical, but his word was good enough for his former chief and I am most grateful. Moreover, as this book goes to press, Jiro Kimura is, I believe, trying hard to persuade Mr. Otani to use my services again to record further reminiscences in this way.

I hope very much that he will succeed. I have been writing about Tetsuo Otani and his family and colleagues for many years now, and it is high time that he spoke for himself. I am delighted that he has agreed to do so at least once, and have done my best to render his informal, unpretentious Japanese into the kind of English that will, I hope, convey something of its flavour, and lend itself to equally colloquial translation into other languages.

JAMES MELVILLE
Bath, Somerset, England,
January, 1991

Chapter 1

LOOKING BACK ON THE WHOLE AFFAIR, I'D SAY THAT NOT only chronologically speaking but also in terms of its significance, the girl in the fake leopard-skin shorts began everything. She and her companion were a yard or two ahead of Hanae and me: the girl about eighteen, I suppose, and her boy friend a year or two older.

Under the shorts she had on pink tights. There were floppy boots on her feet, and above the waist she was wearing a T-shirt with some English words on it. I'd noticed these when she half turned to look behind her for a moment, but of course had no idea what they meant. Kimura tells me that these T-shirt slogans in English that are so popular either make no sense or are obscene, but since the youngsters who buy them don't realise that, it hardly matters.

Her legs weren't all that impressive, to be honest. Otherwise, allowing for her outlandish clothes and peculiar hair-do, she wasn't a bad-looking child. I said as much to Hanae, adding in a perfectly reasonable way that she'd probably look very attractive in a kimono. After all, the young fellow with her actually was wearing traditional Japanese dress and clomping along awkwardly with wooden *geta* on his feet. It's become something of a fad among boys of his generation to get themselves up like that at New Year.

It isn't quite like it was in the old days, when men of the age I am now commonly put on formal rig for the ceremonial outing to one of the big Shinto shrines within easy reach of home. Then, the kimono was the respectable, appropriate thing to wear for the occasion, and meant nothing in particular. The young men who go in for it now tend to be either right-wingers or just show-offs swaggering about for fun. This particular one looked a bit of a thug, as a matter of fact. Anyway, I certainly didn't expect to get my head bitten off for making what was no more than a passing remark, and at first couldn't believe my ears.

"Tetsuo, if you don't stop this I shall leave you, I swear," Hanae said, sounding absolutely furious. Dumbfounded, I turned and looked at her. She'd spoken with fierce intensity but hadn't raised her voice, and I shouldn't think anybody overheard her. All the same, the fact that she had stopped me in my tracks caused quite a commotion.

It was the second of January, you see, and the road leading up the slope to the Ikuta Shrine in central Kobe was closed to vehicles, as it had been on New Year's Day itself, and would be again on the third, to enable tens of thousands of people to make their way into the precincts and approach the sanctuary.

At what you might call peak time during those three days, between about nine in the morning and midafternoon, only a minority manage to get near enough to grab hold of one of the decorated hanging ropes and give it a good shake so as to rattle the tinny bell at the top to attract the attention of the gods. Even so, almost everybody pitches a few coins into one of the cavernous offertory boxes, if necessary over the heads of those jostling in front of them. No doubt they reckon, as I do, that the gods hardly need reminding that they're on special duty at that time of the year.

It's no use trying to force the pace up that approach road: you're part of a human river and you have to go with the

2

inexorable current. So naturally it's troublesome for the people behind when somebody obstructs the flow, as I did, until a tight-lipped Hanae tugged at my sleeve exasperatedly and got me moving again. I could hardly pretend not to have heard her extraordinary outburst, but on the other hand clearly we couldn't have any sort of discussion about it in those surroundings. All I could do as we moved along was edge us both obliquely towards the side of the street. Progress was painfully slow, and I didn't manage to extricate us from the mainstream until just after we passed between the massive orangey-red uprights of the main *torii* gateway and were in the outer precincts of the shrine.

There Hanae followed me to a comparatively quiet little backwater; an untidy corner already half occupied by crates of empty beer bottles. There'd be a lot more there by the end of the afternoon, because most of that side of the open space was taken up by open-air food stalls, the people behind them shouting out cheerful encouragement to potential customers. They were selling the usual snacks: fried noodles, grilled corn on the cob, hot squid shiny with rich, sticky sauce—to which I'm normally very partial on these occasions—lurid red hot dogs on sticks, candy-floss and so on.

It was a lovely morning, I remember, with only a wisp or two of cloud in a pale blue sky, and the air had that perfect clarity you only get in mid-winter. I was greatly troubled by what Hanae had said, but remember having time to think it a great pity that she had chosen this particular time and place to unburden herself. She'd spoiled everything.

"Now then. What's all this about?"

We'd been married for over half my lifetime and more like two thirds of hers, and obviously we'd had our disagreements and snapped at each other often enough over the years. We'd even had quite serious quarrels from time to time, mostly during the period when our only child, Akiko, had been a student at Kobe University and got seriously involved with a bunch of Maoist radicals.

Most often, however, when Hanae's upset or angry with me she gives me the silent treatment, which I must admit

3

is almost invariably effective. I tend to do much the same thing, retreating into myself until the situation sorts itself out one way or another. I can remember only a single occasion when something she said so enraged me that I came terrifyingly close to striking her; and that was in wholly exceptional circumstances. I'd only just got her back after she'd been abducted and I was still in a precarious mental state.

The point I'm making is that, leaving aside the occasional and inevitable ups and downs, Hanae and I get along remarkably well. I doubt if there's a married person on earth who could honestly claim never to have daydreamed about being single again, and I can't think that Hanae is any more of an exception to that rule than I am. Nevertheless, until that day my wife had never, even in jest, so much as hinted at the possibility of leaving me, and I was having great trouble in handling what she'd said.

Looking at Hanae, most people would probably sum her up as a typical, comfortably off, middle-class Japanese housewife in her fifties. The more observant would note the intelligence in her eyes and would guess that she took a lively interest in things. All the same, they'd most likely see her as a conventional sort of lady, her children, if any, grown up and off her hands, and content to run her home efficiently and take unobtrusive care of her husband while indulging in some suitable pastime such as calligraphy, cookery or classes in English at the local women's association.

In spite of everything that happened subsequently, on the whole I still think they'd be right. Hanae was a child during the war, but she's quite old enough to remember what it was like to go cold and hungry in the bitter years that followed the surrender. The quiet strength in her was no doubt partly inborn, but it was also forged by experience, and by her upbringing. In her young days girls were conditioned to accept without complaint the traditional role of respectable Japanese women of all classes, and not to waste time hankering after the unattainable.

4

Things were already getting easier by the time we were married, and continued to improve. My own police career went pretty well, and with promotion came better pay, at a time when there were more and more things to be bought in the shops. Ours was an arranged marriage but we liked each other from the first, and after a period of newly-wed awkwardness found great delight in physical love. So much so that it wasn't long before Hanae began to tease me about my poker-face and I discovered with pleasure that I could make her laugh. In order to do my job I have to be sober and dignified in public. In private, though, we've always enjoyed ourselves a lot and I haven't had to try very hard to respect her and think of her as a person and not just as a housekeeper, sexual partner and the mother of my child. Yet now, this woman I thought I knew so well stood there beside the crates of empty Kirin beer and Fanta soft drink bottles, a look of cold, settled hostility on her face.

"What is this all about?" I repeated. "About leaving me if I don't stop. Stop what, for heaven's sake?"

Hanae met my stare unflinchingly for a few seconds before slowly shaking her head from side to side. When she did speak it was with frigid politeness, almost as if I were a stranger who'd offended her in a public place.

"It's incredible, but I can only assume you really don't know. So I shall have to enlighten you. You got up at about half past seven this morning, and it's now nearly ten. During the past two and a half hours you have done nothing but grumble and complain. About the picture on the breakfast cereal packet. About something or other you heard on the radio news. About my sister Michiko. About having to put on a decent suit to come here and then, on the train, about the fact that a lot of people have decided to wear casual clothes to visit the shrine. About those Christians waving their anti-Shinto placards about—"

"Now hold on a minute," I protested, clutching at a straw, "I said they were a miserable bunch of killjoys with faces like pickled plums, and you agreed with me."

"Yes, I know I did and as a matter of fact I still do, but

5

that's not the point. The point is that during the past few months *you* have turned into a miserable killjoy yourself. An arrogant, intolerant and thoroughly disagreeable man, in fact. When I heard you being gratuitously offensive about that perfectly innocent girl in front of us, I suddenly realised that I can't cope any longer with what you seem to have become. I've tried to make allowances, I know you've had your problems at the office, but . . ."

Hanae's voice had begun to waver and she didn't finish the sentence. She closed her mouth but her lips went on working. I could see that she was very close to tears, and at the same time horrified to think that she might be about to break down in public. In a strange way this helped me to contain my own fury, even though my heart was pounding irregularly and my palms were wet with sweat. I wanted to shout and swear, smash something, and did in fact grab violently at Hanae's arm, casting a wild glance around and by chance catching the eye of an old woman presiding over a nearby stall selling *amazake*, the hot sweet drink like thin gruel. It's made from *sake* lees and smells vaguely alcoholic, but I imagine you could drink a bucketful without getting even slightly tight. It is somehow comforting, however, and tastes quite good in winter.

The old girl nodded at me and beckoned with what she must have thought was an inviting smile. I was more in the mood for a stiff whisky, but without thinking much about what I was doing I dragged Hanae over to one of the low benches provided for customers to sit on and shoved her down on to the strip of red felt laid on top, telling her to sit down and shut up. It was probably the most sensible thing I could have done. Stoking up her anger again by treating her harshly seemed to bring Hanae back from the brink, and incidentally calmed myself down enough to go and pay for a couple of beakers of the steaming *amazake*. I was still in a state of turmoil, though, and managed to mutter no more than a word or two in response to the incessant chatter the old lady kept up while she laboriously plied her ladle and topped off the drinks with grated fresh ginger.

I carried the beakers of *amazake* over to where Hanae was sitting bolt upright on the bench, and offered her one which she took and sipped in stony silence. I drank mine standing up. It was at least a couple of minutes before either of us spoke, and then Hanae just beat me to it.

"Well?"

"Well what?"

"Haven't you anything to say?"

"No. You started this, not me, Ha-chan."

She compressed her lips and glared at me. It made a change from wooden expressionlessness, but not for the better. "Please don't call me that," she said abruptly. She had to mean "Ha-chan," my pet name for her for decades, and being forbidden to use it hurt me more than anything else she'd said so far. My mouth felt dry and sour, and my defensive reaction was to stand on my dignity. I flung my plastic beaker in the direction of a trash bin and pretended not to notice that it missed the target, then straightened my shoulders.

"As you wish," I said curtly. "And since you find my company so disagreeable I won't continue to inflict it on you today. I'll go into headquarters and do some work."

Hanae stood up and responded with equal formality. "Very well. We should talk about this properly, though. In private."

"I agree. When I hope I may find you in better humour. I take it you're not planning to pack your bags today?"

"Don't be ridiculous. I shall expect to see you at home this evening." And with that, Hanae simply turned and walked away from me without so much as a backward glance, heading towards the shrine's much less busy side entrance.

I stood there for a minute or two like an idiot, utterly desolate and wondering how on earth a casual remark of

7

mine about a girl in the crowd could have led to such an explosion of bitter, pent-up hostility. I was at the same time angry and offended myself. Regrets began to nibble at the edges of my fine fury a little later, when I realised I'd reacted like a sulky child to what must have been a cry from the heart, snapping at her in return and turning what might have been no more than a tense moment into an undeniable crisis.

Five minutes after that I was telling myself that I should have chased after Hanae, offered some sort of truce and taken her off to one of the luxury hotels to talk the problem through quietly over coffee. Too late, of course. By the time I did stir myself she had been swallowed up by the crowd and I had condemned myself to spend the rest of the holiday alone with my sour thoughts. So it seemed to me at that moment, anyway.

Eventually I shuffled aimlessly back into the moving crowd, which conveyed me like a piece of human flotsam towards the front of the sanctuary. There I stood for a while gazing vacantly at the dozens of huge bottles of *sake*, mountains of pounded rice cakes and other offerings piled up on the polished wooden steps beyond the lattice-topped chests in which not only coins but also banknotes of every denomination were heaped high. Robed priests were moving about inside doing whatever it is they do on these festival occasions, apparently oblivious to the incessant racket of the bells, the flashing of hundreds of cameras and the occasional hollow booming of a drum.

All at once I became sick of the noise, the pushing and jostling, and the oppressive proximity of so many people. I forced my way out to one side, but couldn't face the idea of fighting my way back against the tide, so I followed the path that ran along the blind side of the main sanctuary building towards the rear. There were a good many people about there too, but nothing like the crush in front.

I was acting without conscious thought, but in retrospect

8

I realise it was a good thing that I went that way. If I hadn't, it's very unlikely that I should have set eyes on Hideki Suminoe before he was murdered.

Chapter 2

THERE'S A SEASONAL PATTERN TO POLICE WORK. FOR EXAMple, the second half of December's always busy. Practically every employed person in Japan goes to one or more of the so-called forget-the-year parties that mean big business for restaurants; and the whole point of taking part in those occasions is to give one's inhibitions an evening off. So a good many normally respectable salarymen find themselves cooling off in the cells for an hour or two after letting their hair down too enthusiastically. There's generally something of a peak in the suicide statistics just before the turn of the year, as well. A lot of older people seem to decide they just can't be bothered to embark on another twelve months.

By contrast, virtually the entire population is usually on its best behaviour during the first three days of the New Year when all the factories and offices are closed, so that police don't as a rule have all that much to do. In fact, the only officers under my command who can always expect to be fully stretched over the holiday period are those whose job it is to see the traffic, both pedestrian and vehicular, keeps moving reasonably smoothly. Needless to say, we have to remain effectively manned in all the operational departments and make standby arrangements to cope with any eventuality, but I like to encourage as many people as can be spared to take a few days off at this time.

Of the three immediate subordinates I most rely on, Kimura never needs much persuading to take time off. When he'd put in an application for a full week's leave I approved it at once, quite expecting him to announce that he'd see me when he got back from France, or Italy, or perhaps America where he had after all been born and partly brought up. I was quite surprised when he said he planned to go to Tokyo for a few days, and assumed he'd decided it was time to look up one or more of his smart lady friends there.

Ninja Noguchi comes and goes more or less as he pleases anyway, and with my blessing. I doubt if he remembers what an official leave application form looks like, and he must have accumulated months of unused entitlement. Even after all these years I don't have much of an idea how he spends his free time, and he certainly wouldn't appreciate my enquiring. I supposed he'd be mooching about Kobe or Osaka somewhere, probably betting on the horses or at the bicycle races.

That left Inspector Takeshi Hara, who had been transferred from Nagasaki a few years before to succeed poor crazed Sakamoto as head of criminal investigation, and who had volunteered to act as senior day duty officer from the first to the third of January inclusive. When I wandered into headquarters myself a couple of hours after the traumatic scene with Hanae it was with the intention of avoiding him if at all possible, but I ought to have realised that this was a vain hope. After exchanging New Year greetings with the young policewoman on duty at the reception desk in the lobby, I told her that I was only looking in and wouldn't be long, but she must have passed the word around that the Old Man was on the premises. I'd been in my own office lackadaisically turning over a few papers for no more than ten minutes when I heard a discreet tap on my door. As soon as I called out to whoever it was to come in, Hara seemed to materialise in the room.

11

"Shinnen omedeto gozaimasu!" he said formally, bowing low.

"And a happy New Year to you too, Hara-kun. Lovely morning. Everything ticking over all right?"

"Nothing out of the ordinary so far, sir, I, um, hadn't expected to see you until the day after tomorrow."

"If it comes to that, I'd no intention of coming in. But then I found myself in the vicinity and thought I might as well fill in a couple of hours." I tried to make it sound casual, but in fact I was all too aware that Hanae had announced that she didn't expect me to go back to the house until the evening, and was wondering how on earth I was going to occupy myself in the meantime.

Hara's in his thirties: a bulky man. Not beefy in the sense of being athletic-looking, but much taller than I am, and well covered. He wears glasses with circular lenses and metal frames that strike me as being of an old-fashioned design but which I'm told are in fact the latest thing. He's a clever fellow, quite the intellectual in fact, and on duty he affects a pedantic manner that used to irritate me a lot until I got to know him better.

"I see." There was a quizzical expression on Hara's big moon face that made it quite obvious that he wasn't taken in by my pose of nonchalance, but was in fact very curious about the reason for my unexpected appearance on such a day. Kimura or Noguchi would have been just the same; wondering why on earth I wasn't with Hanae, either at home or out somewhere, perhaps over on Awaji island with our grandson Kazuo and his parents.

I knew I was being clumsy, but now that Hara had turned up I was glad of his company and didn't want him to go. I got up from my chair and went over to the low table with the black easy chairs grouped round it that we always used for meetings of what we'd all come to refer to rather pretentiously as my inner cabinet. "Come and sit down, if you can spare a couple of minutes."

After hesitating for a few seconds Hara joined me, as

12

usual perching himself on the edge of his seat like a nervous candidate at a job interview.

"I've just come from the Ikuta Shrine," I told him. "Masses of people there, as you'd expect. I was in luck though. I wandered through to the back of the sanctuary and spotted something going on in a small enclosure in a quiet corner of the precincts. Ordinary people weren't allowed in, but there weren't all that many in the vicinity anyway, and I had a good view when I went up to the barrier."

"Indeed, sir?" Hara sounded bored, and I'm quite sure he must have been wondering why on earth I was babbling such banalities. Still, he pricked up his ears a bit when I went on, as I'd guess he would.

"It turned out to be some kind of Noh performance, but unlike anything I've ever seen before. There were a couple of rows of men in the formal costume the chorus always wear, fans and all, sitting on little folding stools. And a flute player and a drummer. And there was one in spectacular brocade robes and with an unusual headdress, the kind you see courtiers wearing in medieval paintings . . . or *sumo* referees, come to think of it . . ." I paused when Hara started nodding his head, waiting to get a word in.

"Yes, yes, of course. He was the master of the Kanze school of Noh. And if you stayed to the end—"

"I certainly did. It was quite interesting."

"I'm sure it must have been. Then what you saw, sir, was a solemn ritual purification and blessing of a particular, greatly treasured Noh mask by a senior Shinto priest—"

"That's right. There were two or three priests and a couple of shrine maidens there. I can't remember which of them untied the silk braids round the box and took the mask out, but it was done with tremendous ceremony. Then after the chief priest had waved his *sakaki* branch over it, one of the Noh fellows helped the man in the robes to put it on—"

"Whereupon he performed part of *Okina*."

"Oh, is that what it was? He shuffled about a bit and

13

kept stamping on the ground. And he was chanting, but that heavy wooden mask tied to his face made it impossible for me to make out any of the words. It wasn't much like any other Noh play I've seen. Not that I've seen very many, I must admit."

Hara looked slightly shocked at my philistine remarks. As a matter of fact I'd already found out more or less what had been going on at the shrine, by asking the knowledgeable-looking man who was standing next to me and closely following every move. In this respect he was unlike most of my fellow-spectators outside the enclosure who were gossiping to each other, taking photographs or hoisting small children up so that they could have a look too. My neighbour had been civil enough and given me a succinct explanation, but he wasn't exactly chatty. Indeed he rather pointedly turned away after a while so I still had questions. The free show I'd seen had distracted my mind for half an hour from the trouble with Hanae, and picking Hara's brains about it was as good a way as any of continuing to plod across the desert of my day. I knew that Hara was something of a Noh enthusiast, and guessed that he'd be well informed.

"Well, sir," he began carefully, "I should perhaps explain that *Okina* isn't a Noh play as such. It is a set of ancient chants and dances rarely performed except at New Year. It isn't surprising that you found the chanting unintelligible. Some of the words are so old that their original meanings have been forgotten. However, it's generally accepted that the whole sequence in itself constitutes an elaborate purification ritual, and at the same time a prayer for the peace and prosperity of the nation."

"I see. Well, nobody's going to quarrel with that, I hope. How do you know it must have been the master of this particular school ... Kanze, you said? There are several others, I know that much."

"Yes. Four others, actually. The Kongo school is dominant in Kyoto. The Kanze theatre and headquarters are in Tokyo."

"Really? He's a long way from home, then. Why would

14

he come all the way from Tokyo to perform at the Ikuta Shrine here? It's not even the most important one in the city."

"It is customary for the masters of the various schools to travel at this time of the year, sir. In response to invitations to visit and encourage their local groups of affiliated amateur enthusiasts. While you were speaking I remembered hearing some time ago that the Kanze master would be coming to Kobe."

"Ah. So the others, the chorus and musicians, I mean, they weren't professionals, then?"

"No. Rather the reverse, in a manner of speaking. They will have been put to considerable expense to experience the privilege of participating in a performance involving the hereditary master himself. There are very few full-time professional Noh players, and it's an expensive hobby for amateurs."

Actually, I'm not as ignorant about Noh as I was pretending to be. Certainly I didn't remember ever having seen or heard about this strange *Okina* piece before, but my old father was something of a Noh fan for most of his life. I don't mean he ever fancied himself as a performer, but he used to take the train from Osaka to Kyoto two or three times a year to attend programmes at the Kongo theatre there, and always took copies of the texts of the plays with him. Now and then he'd bring home a new addition to his pretty comprehensive collection, bought at the theatre. Father took me with him a few times when I was a boy before the war, but I was inclined to fidget and spoil his pleasure.

Anyway, I remembered him telling me more than once that the Noh theatre had always been an expensive business, surviving only through the patronage of aristocrats in the old days, and by charging the earth for tickets in more recent times. So it made sense to me that, as Hara was implying, performances nowadays would be given mostly by and for committed amateur enthusiasts.

That being so, it would certainly be the Japanese way not

only to make them pay through the nose for their own tickets, but also to expect them to bully their friends and relatives into buying some too. When people go on about the austere spirituality of Japanese culture I always think to myself that although he's out of fashion nowadays Karl Marx got it right: everything boils down to economics really. We Japanese are experts at pretending to despise material values while extracting money from the pockets of our fellow-citizens in an ostentatiously high-minded way.

"So one way or another, it seems I should consider myself lucky to see a free show," I said to Hara. "It did strike me that the dozen or so men in the chorus and the musicians all looked like pretty solid citizens. The sort I run across at various Rotary clubs." I cleared my throat in some embarrassment, it having dawned on me as I spoke that Rotary was yet another subject I must have been sounding off about to Hanae altogether too often.

The thing is, the New Port Hotel where my own Kobe South club used to meet was demolished last year. They're putting up some fancy so-called New Hyogo Cultural Hall on the site, and we Rotarians have been dispossessed. The committee are allegedly hard at work finding us a suitable new permanent base for our weekly luncheon meetings, but they're certainly taking their time over it. In the meantime we're making do at the Oriental Hotel, and I often make up my attendance record by dropping in at other Rotary clubs in the city.

"Quite," Hara said. I don't think he approves of such elitist societies.

"All the same, I didn't recognise any of them. They'd definitely have been local people? From the Osaka-Kyoto-Kobe triangle?"

"Apart from the master and perhaps one or two of his personal assistants, undoubtedly."

"There was one who particularly caught my eye. In his sixties, a heavily built, jowly sort of man. A fidget. He didn't seem to be able to sit still like the others, or melt into the background. It was as though he'd have given a lot

16

to be the centre of attention instead of the master. The others sat there like two rows of Buddha images, but even so I got the impression they weren't any more pleased with him than the fellow standing beside me: he kept shaking his head and making exasperated noises."

Hara's normal manner is very solemn, and I've hardly ever seen him smile. He did so then, and I'd forgotten how much more approachable it makes him. "Ah, that must have been Suminoe-san. He fits your description perfectly, both as to his physical appearance and his look-at-me-aren't-I-clever style."

I was surprised. "You know him?"

"He's notorious."

"Well, *I've* never heard of him," I said, rather nettled.

"In Noh circles, that is. Unfortunately I haven't the time or the means to take lessons in chanting or get personally involved, but I do go to performances when I can. I take an interest in Noh."

"Among other things," I said sourly, and immediately wished I hadn't. I'd been trying to carry on as normal a conversation as possible and was genuinely mildly curious about what I'd been watching earlier, but the wretched row with Hanae at the shrine had left me in a very depressed frame of mind, and it had been an error of judgement on my part to try to turn Hara's courtesy call into a lengthy conversation. Being with him reminded me that, as my wife had pointed out, one of the subjects I'd touched on in the course of my litany of grumbling over breakfast had been her younger sister Michiko.

Hanae is proud of Michiko, and justifiably so. Women who achieve the rank of full professor in national universities in Japan, let alone while still in their forties, are very rare birds indeed. The problem for me was that my sister-in-law was having an affair with Inspector Hara, ten years her junior. All very well for Professor Michiko Yanagida: she'd never married and was perfectly free to sleep with any willing adult she chose. Moreover, I have to admit that

17

since she and Hara had fallen for each other, Michiko had been very much nicer to know than before.

The snag is that Hara's married, with two young children, he's a senior officer under my command, and his behaviour is something I can't possibly approve of officially. So I have to pretend not to know what's going on virtually under my nose; but Hara knows that I know, and . . . well, I need not labour the point. He gave me a shifty look which I returned, but sensibly we both drew back from the brink.

"So this Suminoe man is a prominent local Noh enthusiast, and notorious, you say. Notorious for what? Tell me about him, would you?"

"Hideki Suminoe is still titular chairman of the board of the computer software company he founded, and a director of at least one other, but in practice he's more or less retired. He can afford to be, having made a fortune in the late seventies and early eighties. And for the same reason he can well afford to indulge his passion for Noh. In fact he's an extremely generous patron, but you're right in guessing that he isn't popular among other active amateurs. He's vain about his own skills as a performer, and is for ever sponsoring himself as a *shite*. Lead actor."

"Sponsoring himself?"

"Yes. I mean, he's quite capable of putting up all the money for the use of the theatre and hire of back-stage helpers, and then buying up all the surplus tickets and handing them out free to his acquaintances. There are plenty of reasonably well-to-do amateurs, but nobody else around here with money to throw away like that. Suminoe has a big personal collection of costumes and masks, so he can provide his own, too."

"A strange man by the sound of him. Why do the others encourage him?"

"Well, it gives them a chance to perform in public too, which isn't all that easy to arrange. Even if the audiences for a Suminoe appearance are something of—"

"A rag-bag?"

"Well, yes—"

18

"Have you ever seen him do his stuff?"

"Yes, twice. I'm no connoisseur, but even I could see that he's far below professional standard. On the other hand he didn't make a complete fool of himself. He lacks the physical discipline that usually comes from a lifetime of training, but he does have natural authority and an impressive stage presence."

By then Hara was beginning to fidget himself, and in any case I wanted to be alone with my bleak thoughts again. So I changed the subject by asking him how one of his young detectives was getting on with a tricky undercover assignment that entailed his associating with a number of people who might know more than they should about the plans of some of the radical hotheads still lurking about Kobe. Satisfactorily, it seemed, but Hara avoided going into detail.

So after another minute or two I brought the conversation to an end, filing away the information I'd gleaned about Hideki Suminoe in one of the remoter corners of my mind.

I couldn't have imagined at the time how soon I should have occasion to retrieve it.

Chapter 3

I LEFT HEADQUARTERS SOON AFTER MY CONVERSATION WITH Hara and wandered about aimlessly for an hour or so, feeling wretched. The time that had passed since my wife's outburst had done nothing to lessen the shock of hearing her speak as she had, and I realised that I must take a long, cold look at myself. I'm not by nature an introspective sort of person, and this was a difficult exercise for me. I prefer analysing other people's personalities and trying to work out what makes them tick. Being inclined to do that, I now told myself, was *prima facie* evidence of a pretty serious case of self-satisfaction; and what after all had I got to be so pleased with myself about?

In the eyes of the world I was undeniably a man of some consequence, as head of one of the largest provincial police forces in Japan. When I visited England years ago, one or two of the senior British police officers I met were puzzled by what they thought was my comparatively modest rank of superintendent, and I'd had to explain that in Japan superintendents come in a number of different sizes. Like American generals, even down to the insignia we wear.

The top policeman in Japan is the Commissioner General of the National Police Agency, who wears five gold Rising

Suns on each shoulder of his uniform. As a national civil servant, along with half a dozen of my most senior subordinates at headquarters in Kobe and the men in charge of the large divisional police stations, I'm technically a member of his staff. The nine thousand or so other officers in the force I command are employees of the Hyogo prefectural government. The Commissioner General's deputy at the NPA and the Superintendent-General of the Tokyo metropolitan police come next in the national pecking order, each with four stars. I'm a three-star general, as it were: a superintendent supervisor. My English colleagues were quite impressed by that, and told me I'd be called a chief constable in their country.

So I'm something of a VIP, I suppose. Moreover, in fairness to myself I must say that I've cracked some tricky cases during the course of my career. Often by bending the rules, mind you, and even in recent years I've more than once been summoned to Tokyo to be ticked off. Usually following a complaint by the district prosecutor or some other aggrieved local official. Still, I haven't been a bureaucrat myself for all these years without learning a trick or two, and have always been able to talk myself out of serious trouble. Moreover, I was overdue for retirement, carrying on only at Tokyo's request and consequently pretty well fireproof at the time.

All right then, I was a big shot with a good record; but what did my staff think of me? That wasn't something I'd thought about much. I do believe you get the best out of people if you treat them decently. If only for that cynical reason it's good management practice to do so, therefore, and I'm particularly careful to be courteous towards less senior officers, and the civilian support staff I meet.

My relationships with my immediate, day-to-day colleagues are inevitably more complex and personal, and more prone to ups and downs. I failed miserably with former Inspector Sakamoto, now languishing in a secure mental hospital, poor fellow. Since it turned out that he was off his head anyhow, I'm not so silly as to suppose that it

21

was my coldness towards him that drove him to commit murder. Nevertheless I could and should have made much more of an effort to treat him civilly and to conceal my personal dislike of him.

To a much lesser extent I very nearly made the same mistake with Sakamoto's successor Hara when he was first transferred to my command from Nagasaki. I didn't take to him at all, but thank goodness he hit it off right away with Ninja Noguchi, and before long established a good relationship with Kimura too. I have enough respect for their judgement to have accepted that my own first impressions of Hara must have been hopelessly mistaken, and now, in spite of this business with my sister-in-law, I have a lot of time for him.

I often tease Kimura about his fancy clothes, his women and his really quite innocent vanity, but he knows how much I value his remarkable skills, and takes it in good part. As for Noguchi, well, I've often upset him and he's been royally angry with me sometimes, but he's one of my oldest friends, a tower of strength to me, and he knows it. I hope I don't delude myself in believing that I'm held in real, if exasperated, affection by them both.

Hanae's bitter words put all that and much more in question, however. Had I changed a great deal for the worse recently? It's certainly true that as I get older I find that a lot of things get on my nerves; and I'm ashamed to admit that I can work myself up into a fine old state of indignation about the oddest things.

Take the new consumption tax, for example, three per cent on virtually everything you buy. Everyone's up in arms about the principle of the thing. Nevertheless, in quite a few restaurants and other places dealing in relatively modest amounts of money per transaction the tax has been quietly absorbed, much as the increasing popularity of credit cards has forced traders to pay the levies involved. Others have no doubt adjusted their prices upwards a bit, but been sensible enough not to start presenting their customers with bills involving an odd two or three yen. In fact, before the

22

new tax was introduced one hardly ever had to bother with one-yen coins, irritating, weightless and practically valueless little things that they are.

Now in my case, it isn't the tax itself that I mind. Three per cent extra isn't exactly a crushing burden for most people. No, it's having to cope with those fiddly little coins that keep accumulating in lumpy heaps in a jacket pocket. An ordinary domestic postage stamp used to cost sixty yen, and had done for ages, but now it's gone up. Not to sixty-five or even seventy, but to sixty-*two*. When I mention it, people always agree with me that one-yen coins are maddening. All the same, when I thought about it during my walk I realised that this trivial nuisance had developed into something of an obsession with me, and that I must be a total bore on the subject.

I forced myself to face the fact that I was becoming— had already become, according to Hanae—a tetchy, disagreeable old man, with hardly a good word to say for anything new or out of the ordinary. Such as those nauseating, perpetually grinning foreigners who've learned how to chat fluently in Japanese and turn up on the television all the time. *Gaitare*, people call them. Short for *gaijin tarento*: foreign talent. Circus animals would be a better description. Always Westerners, needless to say, Americans or Europeans. Plenty of south-east Asians speak perfect Japanese, but they wouldn't amuse the great viewing public in the slightest. I tried to remember how often I'd aired my views on *that* phenomenon to Hanae, and would have blushed if I'd known how to.

Michiko's affair with Hara was another sore point, and Hanae was quite right to object to my going on about it. Not only was it obvious that she couldn't do a thing to alter the situation, but as matter of fact she'd made it plain from the first that she was happy for her sister. Moreover, she strongly suspected that my disapproval was in great part due to the difference in the ages of the two parties: that I thought Michiko was a cradle-snatcher. The trouble about that is that I can't altogether deny it. I am in many ways

23

old-fashioned and illogical. A relationship between a man and a woman ten years his junior strikes me as being natural and unremarkable, but when it's the other way round it does bother me, no matter what feature articles in *Croissant* have to say about it.

Most men have never come across *Croissant*. The magazine isn't intended for them, and Hanae had probably been buying it for at least a couple of months before I idly looked through a copy I found in the living room and realised that I'd noticed its peculiar name before, out of the corner of my eye as it were.

At first sight it seemed to contain what I think of as the usual mix of articles likely to interest women, fashion and so forth. Then I started reading an article—by a woman, naturally enough—about women members of the National Diet, and was quite struck by its tone. There was a kind of thoughtful passion about it that impressed me.

So I sampled some of the other articles. There was a profile of a middle-aged woman, divorced, who ran her own all-female interpreting and translation agency and was doing well. She hadn't started it as a feminist enterprise and had at first had both women and men on her books; but experience had convinced her that men simply couldn't cope with the idea of having a female boss, so she got rid of them. I remembered having a perfectly amicable conversation with Hanae about the magazine at the time. She told me that it's very popular among women in their thirties and forties, and that the phrase "*Croissant* Woman" was going the rounds.

On that occasion at least I'd had the tact not to point out that she herself was old enough to be the mother of a *Croissant* woman at the lower end of that age scale, and I was more amused than anything else by the idea that my gentle, understanding Hanae was fantasising over articles about female high-flyers.

I'm digressing. In the course of my wanderings I'd reached Meriken Park near the harbour, and in spite of my preoccupations was feeling hungry. I considered the options open to me. I could go home to Rokko with my tail between my legs and face the chilly reception it seemed certain I'd get there. Or I could find something to eat and think about ways of putting off the evil moment by going to see a movie or something. Even on the second of January a few places would be bound to be open in the huge Sannomiya underground shopping mall. It seemed to me on balance that both Hanae and I would benefit from a lengthy cooling-off interval, so I headed for Sannomiya and the prospect of food.

On the way I decided to make a mental note of some pleasant or amusing things about life in contemporary urban Japan, that I could mention by way of refuting Hanae's accusation that I'd turned into a complete curmudgeon. It was hard to think of anything at first, but by the time I reached the small but pleasant open space beside the city hall on Flower Boulevard it had occurred to me that the city fathers of Kobe have over the past couple of decades shown themselves to be uncommonly interested in naked women. I must have passed at least half a dozen pieces of sculpture, provided in the course of the long-running campaign to beautify our streets, and, do you know, every last one of them either included or consisted of a female nude. Very pleasant to look at they were, too.

That, I distinctly remember thinking, was something I could tell Hanae I heartily approved of. Then almost at once I realised that if I were to do so she could use it as ammunition herself. Her sister Michiko undoubtedly would. Typical male chauvinism, she'd snap. Drooling over representations of women as sex objects. Even though, judging from appearances, she was thoroughly enjoying being the object of Hara's sexual attentions.

I don't know why I happened to be thinking so specifically in terms of ammunition in that place and at that time, but I was to discover subsequently that I wasn't the only one. All I felt was a violent blow in my back that knocked me clean off my feet, and then everything went black.

Chapter 4

So Hanae had more time to consider her position, as they say, than we had bargained for when we parted so unhappily at the Ikuta Shrine. When we next met—in the early evening of the same day, I was to be informed—it was in circumstances neither of us could have envisaged in the morning. Whether or not she had come to any significant conclusions by then I can't say: I had personally not been in a position to give much thought to our marital problems since leaving the little park, being unconscious for most of the time.

When I first came to, if you can call it that, I had no idea where I was or what had happened to me. I seemed to be struggling to surface from the depths of a boundless sea of pain; while at the same time to be bound and imprisoned in some terrifying way.

The first, appalling thought I remember having was that somebody had wrongly decided I was dead, and that I had been put into a coffin ready for cremation. It was so dreadful that it must have galvanised my brain into something like proper activity, because I was able to tell myself almost at once that it couldn't be so. For I realised that I wasn't in the more or less foetal position in which Japanese corpses are conventionally arranged in our roughly cube-shaped coffins. I was lying full length in a prone position.

That helped a little, but not much; so with more of an effort than it had ever previously cost me in my life I forced myself to open my eyes. At first I could make no sense of what I saw, and in any case everything was ballooning in and out of focus. After a while, however, I was able to deduce that I was lying on a bed, looking downwards through the end of its frame towards a section of highly polished vinyl tile flooring. Then I became aware of that unmistakable cocktail of aromas that told me I was in a hospital. This was profoundly reassuring. Clearly I was accepted as being still alive, and was not about to be incinerated.

Not that being alive was much fun. I felt ghastly, and couldn't imagine why I was lying face downwards. Nor did I understand why it was impossible for me to move my head, which not only throbbed and ached abominably, but also felt as if it was twice its proper size. While I was trying to work that one out I became aware of the sound of voices in quiet conversation, and then that of a door being opened, and closed again after a couple of seconds.

I must have succeeded in twitching, groaned with pain or otherwise drawn attention to myself in some way, because after what seemed to be a very short time I became conscious of a presence at my side, and could hear various small noises: the rustle of clothing, the clink of glass against metal and so on. It was infuriating not to be able to see what was going on. My mouth felt dry and sour, but after working my tongue round it for a few seconds I managed to croak out a question.

"Who's that?"

"Ah, you're with us again, are you? Good. You're a very lucky man, you know." The voice was cool, cultivated and female; and the remark struck me as being peculiarly inappropriate in the circumstances. True, whatever was happening to me was better than being burned alive, but only marginally, I thought.

"Well, I'm glad you think so," I mumbled, but I doubt if

28

I succeeded in conveying my state of mind to the owner of the voice.

"Yes. You have a remarkably hard head. Concussion, of course, which is why your head's being held in position at the moment; and a colossal lump. But that'll go down in a day or two, and when your hair grows back you'll hardly be able to see the scar where I stitched up the wound for you."

"*You* did?" She'd just told me she had, so it was a stupid thing for me to say, but I'd taken it for granted as soon as she started speaking that she was a nurse. There was a pause, after which the voice wasn't so much cool as icy.

"Yes. Of course, I could have left you bleeding like a stuck pig from your back and with a possible skull fracture while I waited for a male surgeon to arrive, but it's generally accepted that the senior casualty officer—"

"I'm sorry, I didn't mean to—" I began hastily. All I needed at that moment was another touchy woman to contend with.

"So I also extracted the bullet from your back."

"A *bullet*?" It was of course the first I'd heard about a bullet, and I suppose I must have squawked in surprise. After a moment I heard the doctor move, and then her face suddenly came into view not all that far away from my own. I was even more surprised by that, because in order to enable me to see her she was lying on her back on the floor.

"A bullet, yes," she said calmly. "Not the first I've had to deal with, by any means. It made a bit of a mess but didn't do any irreparable damage. I was able to tidy you up reasonably well. Until I saw the X-ray I was a lot more worried about your head than the bullet wound, to tell you the truth."

It was disconcerting to be looking at her sideways on and from such an unusual point of view, but I guessed that she was in her mid-thirties. She had a thin face with sharp features, intelligent eyes and a sardonic expression. By squinting I could just read the name tag clipped to the pocket of her white coat.

"Doctor . . . Sugawara, is it?"

"Excellent. Nothing wrong with your eyesight. Yes, my name is Yoshie Sugawara."

"Well, I'm deeply grateful to you. You must forgive me if I'm not making much sense. I had no idea I'd been shot, you see. I just felt a terrific blow from behind that made me pitch forward, and . . . you can't be very comfortable down there on the floor."

Dr. Sugawara shrugged. "I'm a lot more comfortable than you are, I can assure you. But cheer up, you're not in bad shape for a man of your age, and we shall probably get you on your feet tomorrow. You'll have to sleep face downwards for a while, but you'll be reasonably mobile before long and back at work in a few weeks, I should think."

"How do you know how old I am?" It's odd, isn't it, how in difficult circumstances one often seizes on some quite irrelevant triviality to worry about. Actually, in addition to thinking furiously about the matter of the bullet, I was experiencing a sense of great relief as the reassuring things she'd been saying sank in.

This time she smiled. Briefly, but it lit up her face. "Oh, I know all sorts of things about you. They came as a surprise. The ambulance crew who brought you in had taken it for granted that you were a gangster, you see."

If my head hadn't been hurting so much I'd have laughed out loud at that. As it was, I closed my eyes for a moment and then opened them again. Dr. Sugawara was still lying there, gazing up at me unblinkingly.

"I ask you, do I look like a *yakuza*?"

She pulled a face. "A very senior one, perhaps. One of the barons. And after all, *yakuza* are the only people who usually get shot in Kobe," she said. "But while we were working on you a nurse went through your wallet so that we could identify you. It gave us plenty to talk about, I can tell you. I expect you'd like a drink."

She sat up and then disappeared from view, returning af-

30

ter a short time with a glass of some cloudy liquid with a drinking straw in it. Squatting on her heels, she held it in a convenient position for me. I've no idea what she gave me. It tasted slightly salty but was most refreshing, and by the time I'd sucked it all up I was feeling altogether brighter.

"Thank you very much, Doctor. That's much better. I, er, presume that Hyogo police headquarters have been informed?"

"Naturally." Rather to my disappointment she didn't lie down again, and it turned out that Dr. Sugawara didn't reenter my severely restricted field of vision again that day. She went on talking, though.

"An Inspector Hara wants to come and see you as soon as possible, and he got in touch with your wife. He sent a car to fetch her, I believe. Anyway, Mrs. Otani's outside now. I've told her you're not in any danger. As soon as I've finished with you she can come in for a few minutes, but I'm afraid your Mr. Hara will have to wait until tomorrow morning."

My consciousness had been so dominated by the pain in my head that I'd scarcely noticed the more diffused one emanating from my back, but whatever it was that Dr. Sugawara did to it during the following few minutes quite reversed my order of priorities. She must have pressed a bellpush because another person came into the room after a little while, this time definitely a nurse, and an awkward sort of three-cornered conversation ensued. The two of them swapped incomprehensible technicalities, while from time to time directing the odd remark towards me. I grunted the occasional response, but frankly it was all I could do to prevent myself from howling out loud, and by the time they'd done with me I was in agony. Then, miraculously, it began to abate.

"All finished. And I've injected a pain-killer," the invisible Dr. Sugawara said. "It should take hold any minute now."

"It's beginning to already," I whispered as a hand, pre-

31

sumably belonging to the nurse, appeared before my eyes and dabbed the sweat from my forehead with a wonderfully cool damp cloth. "Thank heavens."

"Fine. Your wife can come in for a while now. Then get some sleep, and I'll have another look at you in the morning."

Both she and the nurse bade me goodnight—the first indication I'd been given of what time it was—and I heard them go out of the room. Then, though I was fast becoming drowsy as the pain continued to ebb away, I heard the door open again, and the voice of Hanae talking to another woman. Not the doctor or the nurse: she was thanking somebody called Migishima-san.

Of course: Woman Senior Detective Junko Migishima. Hara must have sent her along in the car that fetched Hanae from our house. Nice of him, I was dreamily thinking when I felt a light touch on my hand and Hanae's warm breath near my cheek. Then she spoke very softly, not tightly and angrily as when we had parted, but gently and lovingly.

"My poor darling Tetsuo," she said, and I nearly wept. "You must feel dreadful ... but you're going to be all right, Dr. Sugawara says."

I took refuge from the surge of emotion I felt in a feeble attempt to sound nonchalant. "Hello, Ha-chan. I'm glad you've met Dr. Sugawara. She's quite a woman. I'll bet she reads *Croissant* too."

Chapter 5

I WAS MORE ASLEEP THAN AWAKE AND PROBABLY STILL UNDER the influence of the pain-killers when not particularly gentle hands released my head from whatever contrivance had been holding it steady. However, by the time they'd turned me over and eased me up into a sitting position I was only too conscious of what was going on, and I very nearly passed out again when after the briefest respite they got me to my feet and sat me in a wheelchair. The instruction to sit still and breathe shallowly was quite unnecessary—I couldn't possibly have done anything else—but after a few minutes I had to accept that I was a lot better off that way.

A little later I was wheeled from the recovery room and installed in a small private room. That cheered me up. Another encouraging sign was that I felt hungry; not surprisingly in view of the fact that I'd eaten nothing since breakfast the previous day. Normally I enjoy Japanese food at any meal *except* breakfast, preferring to start the day with my regular fare of ham and egg, toast and coffee. Still, I certainly didn't object when they brought me miso soup, a bit of cold grilled fish, rice and pickles. It all tasted marvellous washed down with plenty of green tea, even though I had to manage the chopsticks left-handed, my right arm being out of action. The woman who brought the tray was some sort of auxiliary, not a nurse. She kindly offered to help me eat, especially the rice, but I foolishly turned down the offer and was reduced after she left to scooping it with my fingers. Since nobody was there to see me I didn't care.

Afterwards I had my face washed for me and was shaved. I won't dwell on the other even less dignified details of the way in which I was made presentable and prepared to face the day; especially as, thank goodness, I was able subsequently to take care of myself in those respects. It's enough to say that by the time Hara turned up at about nine I was wearing one of my own *yukatas* that Hanae must have brought with her the previous evening, and sitting bolt upright in the wheelchair. Dr. Sugawara hadn't been to see me yet, but a taciturn nurse had taken a look at my dressings and said they'd do for the present.

"Good morning, Hara-kun," I said bravely enough when he walked in. He stopped short and stared, but I was ready for that, having seen myself in a mirror by then. "Have a good laugh by all means before we get down to business. I know I look like some sort of Indian potentate." The swathes of bandages round my head did look rather like a turban, and I have a pretty swarthy complexion. "Oh, and I'm sitting up straight like this because my back hurts even more if I lean back." I have to hand it to Hara. His mouth worked a bit but he didn't even smile, much less laugh.

In fact he was as punctiliously courteous as I had come to expect him to be, but rather touchingly concerned. He'd been kept informed of my physical condition until late the previous evening and had a briefing from the senior nurse in charge of my case on arrival at the hospital shortly before coming to my room, so we didn't waste too much time on that. What I most wanted were his thoughts on what had happened to me and why, and he duly began with a concise report.

Needless to say, the police automatically get involved when somebody's found unconscious and bleeding profusely from a wound evidently caused by a firearm. A patrolman from the nearby Sannomiya police box had arrived on the scene before the ambulance men took me away, and started questioning the man who'd come to my aid, and various other passers-by who were or who claimed to be witnesses. The patrolman, with a couple of others he summoned by radio to lend a hand, had no idea who I was at that stage, of course. It shouldn't have made any difference if they had, or even if, like the ambulance crew, they assumed that somebody finding himself on the wrong end of a firearm must be a gangster.

So they'd done most of the right things, including making a sketch plan of the immediate area, with an indication of the position in which I'd been found. Not all that much later, the casualty staff at the hospital found my official identification and notified headquarters, so Hara was brought into the picture as a matter of urgency. That is what would have put the whole affair on a different footing. The poor fellows at the Sannomiya police box must have wondered what hit them when Hara descended on them with a carload of scenes-of-crime specialists and took personal charge of the situation.

Well, they gave it the full treatment. Hara had brought with him to the hospital a whole bundle of material to show me: a sheaf of notes, sketches and computations of possible trajectories for the bullet. Not to mention what were to me gruesome colour photographs of the bloodstains I'd deposited on the piece of municipal sculpture that knocked me cold, and on the gravel where I'd ended up. The bullet Dr. Sugawara had dug out of my back—and spoken of rather dismissively, I still thought—had already been identified as having been fired from a hunting rifle.

That was odd. Brooding over what had happened to me, I'd been inclined to suppose that a handgun would have been the weapon used. The sort that doesn't get registered but isn't all that hard to come by if you know somebody and have enough cash. I used to know how to handle a regulation police sidearm but I'm a comparative ignoramus about more sophisticated weapons. Nevertheless, even I

35

know that there's a huge difference in range and accuracy between a handgun and a rifle. The bullet would surely have passed clean through me and out the other side if it had been fired from nearby.

Hara agreed, and after a while we got round to wondering why whoever shot me had chosen to do so when I was in a well-used public open space around mid-day only a hundred metres or so from the busiest intersection in Kobe, with plenty of people strolling about on a major public holiday. Rather than in one of the deserted back streets I'd wandered through, I mean. There must have been plenty of opportunities.

Assuming that I had been the target and that we weren't dealing with some sort of maniac, there seemed to be only two tenable theories. The first—and the one I favoured for fairly obvious reasons—was that wounding rather than killing had been the intention. The known probability that medical help would arrive at such a location within a matter of minutes supported it. So did what Hara then told me, namely that the bullet's point of impact had been well below my shoulder and so far to the right of my spine that it missed the lung. The damage it did was mainly to muscular tissue and one of my ribs. He'd got all that from the senior nurse.

On the other hand it might simply have been that the person with the rifle was a lousy shot. Anyhow, it now seemed that it wasn't the wound that had made me lose consciousness, but the fact that in pitching forward I'd cracked my head against the bronze representation of the nude lady that I'd been contemplating. Nevertheless, my unconsciousness could easily have turned out to be permanent, because I lost a lot of blood even in the short time before the ambulance arrived.

Dr. Sugawara turned up after about forty minutes. She was none too pleased to discover that Hara had been allowed in to see me before she'd had a chance to look me over, and shooed him away at once, telling him in very nearly those words to go and cool his heels for at least half an hour.

I was then made to go and lie face down on the bed again and endure her ministrations, which seemed to take a great deal more than thirty minutes. Eventually, however, Dr. Sugawara declared a truce, informing me once more that I was a very lucky man; and once more I told her bitterly that I was glad she thought so.

Chapter 6

ANYONE WHO HAS EVER BEEN HOSPITALISED CAN EASILY imagine how I passed the next few days, so I'll be brief. The pain from my head wound was the first to retreat and become much more localised, so that provided I was careful not to move my head too quickly it soon ceased to bother me much. My back was another matter. They kept me in hospital for four nights altogether, and between the pair of them, Dr. Sugawara and a brisk male physiotherapist made sure I didn't have a restful time.

I was deprived of the wheelchair after the first day, and made to hobble painfully to and from the bathroom. Moreover, I was also at regular intervals put through a distinctly disagreeable routine of exercises. The physiotherapist was built like a rugger player but told me he was keen on Mozart. He was also quite a joker, claiming that he was starting me off with a few easy, gentle movements just to loosen me up. It felt at first as if he was tearing all Dr. Sugawara's careful needlework apart again. All the same I have to admit that he knew his job, and that before long I'd come round to accepting the cheery official line that I really had been extremely fortunate to have escaped death or—much worse in my opinion—permanent disablement.

I was taken home in an ambulance on the morning of Friday the fifth of January. My back was still strapped up and I had to report to the out-patient department to have it seen to on the following Monday and again on the Thursday of that week, when Dr. Sugawara's repair work in that area too was pronounced to have done its job, and by way of a bonus the stitches in my head were removed. They put a much smaller dressing on the rapidly healing site of the operation on my back, so I no longer looked like an example of work in progress on an ancient Egyptian mummy.

That's all I have to report about my recovery, but needless to say a lot of other things were happening while that was progressing so well. Hanae visited me every day while I was in hospital, and by tacit consent the row we'd had at the Ikuta Shrine was—well, not forgotten, obviously, but avoided as a subject of conversation. I tried my damnedest not to say anything that could be construed as being insensitive, and not to grumble. My conversations with Dr. Sugawara were keeping me up to the mark in the former respect, and I'm glad to say that we got along quite well with each other.

Being careful not to find fault with everything involved surprisingly little effort. Oddly enough, the very unpleasantness of the experience I'd had seemed to have shaken me out of what I now realise had been months of unfocused dissatisfaction with life in general and myself in particular.

Once I was home again, it became more difficult to go on acting as if everything was sweetness and light between Hanae and me, and we did eventually get round to talking briefly but seriously about the situation. That was late on Sunday afternoon, after our daughter Akiko and young Kazuo left to go back to Awaji island. They'd been planning to come over during the holiday period anyway, but Hanae had rung them with the dramatic news about me and put them off for a few days.

So they'd turned up on Saturday and been talked into staying overnight. It was a pity my son-in-law Akira hadn't been able to come too, but with the wholesale markets get-

39

ting into full swing again after the break it was a busy time for market gardeners. Anyway, it was wonderful to see Akiko still so happy with her semi-rural way of life, and my grandson sturdy and inquisitive about everything, including my bandages which impressed him mightily. We went to the gate to see them off, Kazuo walking backwards and waving like mad all the way to the corner of the road.

"Even after that nice Dr. Sugawara told me you were going to be all right I was worried to death about you," Hanae said after a longish silence between us. We were back in the house and she'd seemed restless, moving about and fiddling with things. "But what was almost as bad while you were in hospital and I was on my own here was realising how much I missed you."

I looked into her eyes until my own began to mist over and I had to blink before replying.

"So you've changed your mind about leaving me, then?"

"Did you really think I would?"

"Oh yes, I believed you then, and I think you still might if I don't pull myself together. I've had time to think, during these last few days. I realise I haven't been at all nice to know for a long time now. And I've taken you for granted, which is unforgivable."

We looked at each other again for a long time. Then Hanae hugged me, carefully, so as not to hurt my back, and what we said and did after that is our affair.

Don't run away with the idea that all I had to do that first week was to get back on my feet physically and make peace with my wife. Hara came to see me twice more while I was in hospital, accompanied once by Junko Migishima, whom he had assigned to assist him with my case. I was able to thank her for going to the house and being with Hanae for the first few hours: Hanae had known the young detective for a long time, and her company must have been a comfort.

Ninja Noguchi paid me a touchingly formal visit, wearing a proper suit and scowling with embarrassment as he

40

handed over a box of enormous grapes that must have cost him a small fortune. It reminded me powerfully of the time years ago when our roles had been reversed, and Hanae and I had taken him a melon. It had been a thousand times worse for poor Ninja, who'd been shot—unintentionally, he could cling to that at least—by his own son, who went on to commit suicide. Ninja too must have been reminded of that horrifying experience, because there was a definite awkwardness between us. He mumbled a few words but was obviously disinclined to talk, and very soon made his escape.

Kimura breezed in to see me; on the Thursday, it must have been. Full of beans as usual, he brazenly tried in my presence to make a date with Dr. Sugawara, who turned him down with great good humour. He had a distinctly tonic effect on me, and for all I know he might well have returned to the charge later and talked the doctor into accepting his invitation after all. I reminded Kimura that he was supposed to be on leave and in Tokyo, but of course I knew that he would have come rushing back the moment he heard what had happened. It would have been highly uncharacteristic for Kimura to pass up the earliest opportunity to get in on such a newsworthy affair.

Newsworthy: that is of course the key adjective. It's not often that anybody other than a member of an organised crime syndicate is shot in Japan, and when the occasional innocent citizen does get caught accidentally in crossfire between warring hoodlums, it hits the headlines. Kimura reminded me that there had been no end of a fuss when a stray bullet found its way into a house occupied by an American resident who lived next door to a gang boss, and wrecked his son's radio or video recorder or something like that. Nobody was hurt, but the gangs involved sent deputations to apologise to the American family for their clumsiness, and paid handsome compensation.

So you can imagine what the media made of it when the head of a prefectural police force was shot in the back; especially as the identity of the culprit and the motive were then and were to remain for a long time completely unknown. As it turned out, my sudden fame was mercifully short-lived, because not much more than a week later the national newspaper editors and television commentators forgot all about me in their excitement over the shooting outside his own city hall of Mayor Motoshima of Nagasaki.

There was no doubt who was responsible for that: the man concerned was proud of what he'd done and only too pleased to brag about it. He was a right-wing fanatic who claimed that the mayor, a devout Christian, had insulted the late Emperor in a speech. In fact Motoshima had suggested that the Emperor couldn't be exonerated from any share in the responsibility for what had been done in his name before and during the Second World War; something plenty of other people thought privately but kept quiet about. The mayor had made his remarks some months previously, but the rightists are sticklers for protocol and it wasn't until after the official year of mourning for the old Emperor had ended that the Nagasaki incident took place. It was touch and go for a day or two but the mayor pulled through eventually.

The attack on Mayor Motoshima did at least divert the heat of media attention from me, and its timing gave us food for thought when I decided to put in an informal appearance at headquarters again and sat—most uncomfortably—with Noguchi, Kimura and Hara in my office. That was towards the end of the week after I'd been shot, and the day after the same thing had happened much more spectacularly to the mayor of Nagasaki. I was still officially on sick leave and would remain so until the doctors at our own regional police medical centre pronounced me fit for normal duty, but I was getting restless sitting about at home.

I mustn't give the impression that during my absence my senior colleagues had dropped everything else so as to concentrate on trying to find out who had put me in the hospital and why. The matter had to be looked into, like any other officially reported crime, and the responsibility for that lay with Hara and his criminal investigation section.

Noguchi and Kimura had for some time been working together on a policy for us to adopt in relation to the increasing number of south-east Asian manual workers turning up in Kobe and other cities in the prefecture. It was a national problem, and any amount of paper was coming from Tokyo offering what they had the cheek to call "guidance." The plain fact is that most of these men are in the country illegally, and the authorities are in two minds what to do about them.

Thai, Taiwanese and other south-east Asian *women*—not to mention Americans and Europeans—have been drifting to Japan for decades, of course, and Kimura knows all about them. They work in bars, the former Turkish bathhouses we have to call "soaplands" since the Turkish Embassy kicked up such a fuss, strip-tease shows and so forth. On the whole we've been inclined to turn a blind eye to them. In the nature of things there comes a time when the gangsters who run them import fresh talent, and sooner or later the women mostly leave the country again. Moreover, while they are here they keep pretty quiet.

Illegal male immigrants are another matter entirely. They hope to stay, and as long as we have a shortage of manual labour they'll always be able to wangle poorly paid jobs without too many questions being asked. Presumably the conditions they live under here are an improvement on what they left behind, but they have a wretched sort of life all the same. So not unnaturally they're inclined to get drunk, squabble among themselves and sometimes get involved in murderous fights. In some ways it's getting to be not unlike the situation we faced in the early postwar years, when lawless gangs of Chinese and Koreans roamed about settling old scores and profiting from the general chaos.

One big difference is that in those days the old-style Japanese gangsters were still tightly disciplined, and their bosses regarded themselves as the successors of the tough characters who did in fact keep the peace among the poor in the big cities centuries ago, long before police forces as we know them now were ever thought of. The gang bosses in my young days didn't approve of disorderly behaviour any more than the police did, and quite often lent us a hand. As a green assistant inspector in the late nineteen-forties I was present on one occasion when a mob of armed Chinese hoodlums besieged a divisional police station in Kobe and we were literally rescued by a "task force" of old-style *yakuza* gangsters. Very grateful to them we were, too.

There are still a few *yakuza* barons who pretend to keep up the old traditions, but it's really only in films and on TV that they survive. The Japanese gangster of today isn't about to get involved when a group of fighting-mad Thais quarrel among themselves or pitch into some Vietnamese and the knives come out. Even Ninja Noguchi's inclined to shrug helplessly—which means raising his shoulders a couple of millimetres—when the topic comes up for discussion yet again.

Then there was the general anxiety that filtered down to us from the Public Security Investigation Agency about the increasing boldness of the extreme leftists. Few in number, they're nevertheless clever. They tried to disrupt the funeral procession for the late Emperor. The controversial enthrone-ment ceremonies for the new Heisei Emperor—Kimura tells me that foreigners insist on referring to him by his per-sonal name Akihito which we Japanese would never dream of using—weren't due to happen until November, but there were fears that the radicals were planning something much more spectacular to mark the occasion. The far-right char-acters represented by the fellow who shot Mayor Motoshima weren't likely to stand idly by, so all in all it seemed probable that we were in for a busy year.

It had certainly begun in a lively enough fashion for me, and though I tried to take an intelligent interest in every-thing discussed on that first day I went back, I think I can be forgiven for concentrating particularly on what Hara said when he gave us a progress report about my own case. He

44

looked rather down in the mouth, because in spite of having put a great deal of effort into it and producing a beautifully presented written summary, what he had to say in effect was that he'd got nowhere.

It was Kimura who pointed out the significance of the date of the previous day's attack on Motoshima in Nagasaki, and its relevance to my own experience. The old Emperor died on the seventh of January 1989, and the rightist with the gun had waited until after the year of formal mourning was over before, as he put it, "punishing" the mayor for what he'd said back in the previous October.

"That wasn't just an isolated case, Chief," he said. "We all know that the rightists and the gang bosses who support them have been observing what they call 'restraint' as a mark of respect for the past year. Haven't they, Ninja?"

Noguchi nodded; about as violent a gesture as the shrug I mentioned earlier.

"So my point is that whoever shot you on the *second* of January definitely wasn't a right-wing extremist." Kimura smiled at us all brightly, pleased with himself.

"But right-wingers don't shoot at policemen anyway," Hara put in. "They claim to be upholders of law and order."

"So they do," I said. "But proceeding by elimination is a perfectly reasonable way of tackling this. It's a good point, Kimura-kun. Of course, we're making a very big assumption in supposing that whoever did it had a comprehensible motive at all. He might simply have been off his head . . . I say, Hara, this is interesting!" I'd been idly flipping through his summary of the brief statements taken from the handful of people who'd been in the vicinity when I was hit. "This witness called Suminoe. He isn't by any remote chance the Suminoe you and I had been talking about a couple of hours earlier? The well-to-do Noh enthusiast?"

Hara shook his head. "No, sir. A different given name, and you'll see that the witness gave his age as twenty-seven. Suminoe isn't all that uncommon a family name, after all."

"No. I suppose it isn't. Ah, well."

We went on talking rather aimlessly for a while before I adjourned the meeting, more tired than I cared to admit after a mere two or three hours back in my office. All the same, I couldn't get the name Suminoe out of my head, and decided to make a few private enquiries of my own before calling it a day and going home.

Chapter 7

You might well suppose that I had quite enough to think about one way and another without brooding about a couple of people who both happened to be called Suminoe: the Noh amateur Hara had described as notorious, and the young man who had been nearby when I was shot. I couldn't argue with Hara when he pointed out that the name isn't particularly uncommon, and the assumption had to be that my seeing one Suminoe and being seen by another near the centre of Kobe on the same day was pure coincidence.

Nevertheless, I did spend half an hour browsing through the collection of local directories and general reference books the secretarial staff keep in my outer office, and by checking the listings for computer software companies, I soon tracked down the self-important, twitchy character I'd noticed among the performers at the Ikuta Shrine. Hideki Suminoe, chairman of the board, just as Hara had said. Judging by the published details of his company's capitalisation and the fact that their head office was located in a well-known and extremely fancy building, Suminoe must indeed be well able to afford his expensive hobby.

I wondered where he lived, and tried the phone book

first. They say that Japanese telephone directories are the biggest unread books in the world, and when you consider the problems involved in looking up proper names written in Chinese characters but arranged phonetically, it's not surprising. In the many cases where one can't be at all sure how they're pronounced, that is. Suminoe's not one of the tricky ones, as it happens, but I couldn't find a Hideki among the many listed in the Kobe-Osaka-Kyoto area. I hadn't really expected to. Wealthy business men are inclined to be coy about publishing details of their private addresses and telephone numbers.

With the resources at my disposal, it would have been the easiest thing in the world for me to put one of my staff on to the job of finding out the address of Hideki Suminoe, and virtually anything else I might wish to know about him. Alternatively, I could simply have asked Hara to look into the possibility that there might be some link between him and the twenty-seven-year-old witness. When I'm just playing with ideas, though, I hate showing my hand to anyone. I suppose this is because some of my flights of fancy are so wild and turn out to have been so completely nonsensical that it would be embarrassing to have them exposed to scrutiny.

Anyway, I sat there wondering what to do next, and after a while it occurred to me that though I'd never come across him in that context myself, such a substantial man as Suminoe might very possibly be a Rotarian. It was easy enough to check that. I rang my old friend Fumio Iwai who is a fellow member of my own club. Iwai was a journalist before he rose to fame and fortune as a best-selling novelist and television personality, and he is also a great gossip who knows everybody.

I was in luck. He was at home, and sounded quite pleased to hear from me. Needless to say, he'd heard all about me and the mystery gunman and was all friendly concern, wanting to know how I was and so forth. Having given him a carefully edited account of the way I had spent the morning of the second of January, I was able to mention quite casually that I'd watched the little ceremony at the shrine and learned from Hara the name of the performer who hadn't quite fitted in. I heard Iwai chuckle fruitily, and then go into a fit of coughing.

"You shouldn't smoke so much," I told him while I was waiting for him to get over it. "Anyway, what's so funny?"

"Nothing, really," he wheezed eventually. "It's just so typical. Old Suminoe's such a prima donna. Always has been, even before he had quite so much money to chuck about."

"You're a fine one to talk," I pointed out. Iwai's own image is decidedly bohemian and Kimura, an expert on such matters, tells me he must spend a great deal of money on cultivating it. "Anyway, obviously you know him."

"Well, hardly in a personal sense. Though I did go to his house to interview him once while I was still on the paper. Seven or eight years ago, must have been. One of those big flashy western-style places. In Ashiya, not all that far away from where you live."

This was splendid. Iwai was well away by then, and it only needed the occasional "Really?" or amused grunt from me to keep him going.

During the following few minutes I learned that while the main part of Suminoe's luxurious house was full of state-of-the-art gadgetry, a complete contrast was provided by an austerely beautiful Japanese-style annexe in which he kept his Noh paraphernalia, and where he had on the occasion of his visit subjected Iwai to a tea ceremony accompanied by a tedious lecture on the subject. Much more interesting to me was the revelation that Suminoe was that comparatively rare animal in Japan, a lifelong bachelor; and that he was looked after by a married couple.

"Well, he does have these two nephews," Iwai said when I expressed surprise. "His only close relatives, I believe. Don't get the wrong idea, they're proper nephews, his late brother's sons. You seem to be very curious about all this, Otani-san. Are you up to something?"

"Why ever should I be? You're the one who's been go-

49

ing on about the man." I tried to inject a note of injured innocence into my voice, but might have known that Iwai was too sharp a character to be taken in.

"Yes, I have, haven't I? Because you've been playing your old trick of leading me by the nose. I swear to you, from now on if you so much as ask me what the weather's going to do I shall assume you have ulterior motives. Now pay attention, because I've got to go out in a couple of minutes. One of the two Suminoe nephews is high up on the technical side of the computer business the old chap founded. A computer whiz and a great asset, I gather. No question of his being favoured because of the family connection. The younger one—by about seven or eight years—is altogether different. Has a job as a junior high-school teacher, I seem to recall, but really wants to be a composer, or something like that. Perhaps when Uncle dies he'll be able to afford to spread his wings. Right, satisfied?"

"Almost. How old are these nephews?"

"At a guess, late twenties and mid-thirties. Thereabouts."

"Thanks a lot," I said, and meant it.

"Just one thing before you ring off."

"Yes? I'm listening."

"I shall permit you to pay for my lunch at the next Rotary meeting."

Chapter 8

THE FOLLOWING SUNDAY AT ABOUT TEN-THIRTY IN THE MORN-ing, Hanae's sister Michiko came to see us. By then, I was getting about tolerably well, especially since Hanae had rummaged in the little fireproof store-house behind the house and dug out a handsome black walking stick that had belonged to my father. She polished up its silver top, and to be quite honest I rather fancied myself when I used it. I'd been instructed by the Mozartian physiotherapist at the hospital to go for a walk every day, you see.

It was a fine, sunny day, and after we'd all had a cup of coffee and one of the expensive cakes Michiko always brings when she visits, Hanae suggested that we should leave her to busy herself in the kitchen, and take the air for an hour or so before lunch.

I had mixed feelings about the idea. There was no doubt that since she and Inspector Hara had embarked on their affair, the previously prickly Professor Michiko Yanagida had been more friendly and agreeable towards me than ever before. She had even taken to using my given name, Tetsuo, from time to time, having previously studiously avoided calling me anything at all. Now I may not be quite old enough to be her father, but given that she still invariably calls Hanae "big sister" this was astonishingly bold and un-Japanese, even for somebody as up-to-date and internationally minded as Michiko. Not that I was upset. Quite the reverse; I found it appealing.

On the other hand it was becoming more and more difficult to keep up the ridiculous pretence that I didn't know she was involved with Hara. It was one of those silly "she knew that he knew that she knew" situations, which I felt I had to try to sustain because of my official relationship with her lover. You'll have gathered that I'd recently come very close to having the whole thing out with Hara, so what with one thing and another, being *tête-à-tête* with the new Michiko wasn't a prospect I looked forward to eagerly.

Still, we set out together and chatted amicably enough as we ambled along. The whole district around my house is very hilly, and I was grateful when I noticed that Michiko unobtrusively made allowances for my slowness. I remember pointing out an unusual sight in an area where land for housing is practically worth its weight in gold: a level, fair-sized tract overgrown with a tangle of weeds.

There's an interesting row going on about it, and Kimura of all people is having to keep an eye on the matter. This is because he's our expert on dealing with foreign officialdom, and it seems that the Philippine Embassy in Tokyo holds the legal title to the land. This is disputed by a local developer who could make a fortune by building on the site. Meantime it has turned into a mini-wilderness and a playground for wild boars that come down from Mount Rokko, often in broad daylight. We hung about to see if we could spot one, but gave up after a few minutes and went on.

After a while we reached the big up-market development of apartment blocks known as Rokko Grand Hills, and I was ready for another breather. There's a children's playground attached to the flats, near a small amphitheatre used for open-air shows in the summer, and I thankfully lowered myself on to one of the benches provided there for adults.

"Sorry. I need to sit down for a bit. Do you mind?"

Michiko settled herself beside me. "Of course not. It's pleasant here in the sun."

The playground commanded a spectacular view out to the Inland Sea far below, and more immediately overlooked a deep wooded gully; wickedly dangerous for small children, I should have thought, since it wasn't railed off all that securely. I said as much to Michiko, but she shrugged.

"I doubt very much if the sort of people who live here would let their children play outside without supervision. Look at the way all the dads are hovering over them. Doing their Sunday duty."

It hadn't occurred to me until then that apart from Michiko there wasn't a woman in sight. There must have been well over a dozen youngsters playing, ranging in age from about four up to nine or ten. A couple of them were weaving about on little yellow bicycles adorned with Atom Boy and similar cartoon stickers. The bikes were the kind with little stabiliser wheels on either side, but even so the riders managed to wobble unsteadily. No problem, though. Each was attended by an anxious father with a protective hand outstretched ready to forestall any mishap; while similar youngish men kept a wary eye on the other children who were skipping, bouncing astride big rubber balls with handles or holding those mysterious, earnest conversations that small boys and girls go in for.

"I see what you mean," I said. "They all look alike, don't they? All wearing jeans and sweaters and those peculiar running shoes."

"Trainers. They're called trainers. It must make a pleasant change for salarymen who have to wear boring suits to work every day." Michiko paused, then made a little sound half-way between a snort and a laugh. "You're quite right, though. Swapping one uniform for another doesn't make much sense, does it?" She twisted round on the bench and surveyed me with a tolerant smile. "Well, at least there's very little danger of your becoming a slave to fashion, Tetsuo."

I was wearing an ancient sports jacket, a comfortable

shirt and grey trousers. With respectable footwear and a necktie, naturally. "No. I leave all that sort of thing to Kimura. And of course I'm long past child-watching duty except very occasionally when Akiko authorises young Kazuo to take me out."

Sitting there watching the activity in the playground, it dawned on me that Michiko had her reasons for choosing a Sunday for her visit. Inspector Hara had young children, and was probably clad in natty leisurewear and occupied a few kilometres away in much the same way as these young fathers we were observing. It was all I could do not to make some oblique reference to him, but I bit my tongue. Michiko was no doubt a *Croissant*-reading woman, and there was no point in my going out of my way to needle her. As it happened, she disarmed me by bringing up the subject herself in the next breath.

"I expect they're quite enjoying it. Takeshi admits he does. Makes these absentee fathers feel virtuous, I suppose, even though they only do it for a couple of hours a week, while the mothers are responsible day in and day out."

Michiko seemed to have decided to put an end to the farce, and I agreed that it was high time. "Look, I know your private life is none of my business," I began carefully, "but since you've mentioned his name, I must point out that to a certain extent Inspector Hara is. My business, I mean."

"Indeed? I imagined the police had long since given up looking for evidence of dangerous thoughts." Michiko's far too young to understand the chilling effect the use of that last phrase has on somebody of my generation with lively recollections of wartime; so I took a deep breath and tried to keep calm.

"Hear me out, please. Obviously, I've known about all this since soon after it began last summer."

"And deeply disapproved, because you think I'm a baby-snatcher."

I clenched the fist she couldn't see, trying even harder to keep my temper. "It isn't that. I don't deny that I'm old-fashioned, and just as illogical about that sort of thing as most men, but my private opinions are irrelevant. Hara's married, with children, but that's not the point either. What matters is that he's a senior national civil servant and a member of my staff on whose performance and fitness for promotion I have to report annually."

"So? Anything wrong with his performance? Do you doubt his fitness for promotion in due course?"

"The answer to both those questions is no. But don't you see, the pair of you are putting me in an impossible position? I must either claim to be unaware of his relationship with you, which makes me look a fool when I'm afraid it's becoming more or less common knowledge at headquarters. Alternatively, I must take official note of it before somebody stops him, and either course would be bad for Hara."

"Why?" Michiko sounded genuinely curious, and so far we'd avoided raising our voices. I was hoping we could keep it that way.

"Because if I were to be seen to be tolerating a situation in which one of my heads of departments is having an affair with a close relative of mine, it would look as if I was favouring him. Adultery is neither a crime nor even a serious disciplinary offence these days, though I can assure you that not so long ago it was. Nevertheless, for it to be known that a potential high-flyer like Hara has an openly irregular private life would go down very badly at the National Police Agency."

To my great surprise, Michiko not only laughed out loud, but actually put a hand on my thigh and squeezed it in what I took to be a friendly fashion. I was shocked, and made no attempt to conceal the fact, but spoke as bitterly as I felt towards her.

"You think it's funny, do you? Well, I'm glad you seem so unperturbed."

"I am. And so is Takeshi. I'm afraid you aren't the subtle bureaucrat we took you for."

"*We?*"

"Yes, we. Do you imagine he and I haven't discussed all

55

this? In the first place, you must have gathered through my sister that I haven't the smallest intention of trying to break up his marriage. Not that I'd have much chance of succeeding if I did."

"Well, one must be thankful for small mercies, but I don't see how that alters the situation."

"Oh, but it does. If you heard that your promising young Inspector Hara was having an affair with some other unmarried woman you wouldn't feel obliged, as you pompously put it, to 'take official note' of the situation, would you?"

I resented being called pompous, and tried to strike a cynically humorous note. "Well, no, probably not. Unless it turned out that he'd picked the district prosecutor's sister-in-law, or the prefectural governor's."

Michiko raised her eyes to heaven. "You're persisting in being obtuse. You still haven't grasped the point, have you?"

Pompous *and* obtuse. She was certainly being frank enough. I raised open hands in a gesture of surrender, dropping my important walking stick in the process. "Very well, I give up. Enlighten me. What *is* the point?"

It needed a considerable effort for me to retrieve the stick, but she just sat and watched, not making the slightest attempt to help.

"The point, Tetsuo, is that I'm *not* a relative of yours, any more than the sisters-in-law of the district prosecutor and the governor are relatives of theirs."

I thumped myself on the forehead. Of course. There was no need for her to go on after that, but I let her, while I recovered from my exertions.

"By marrying you, the former Hanae Yanagida became a member of the Otani family, and her name was duly struck off our household register. *She* is a close relative of yours. But I'm not legally a relative at all, and I suggest you point that out to any busybodies in Tokyo who take it upon themselves to poke their noses into our business."

Well, she was technically right, and as a matter of fact

that argument would probably prevail if I were ever to be taken to task and be obliged to fall back on the fine print of the police service regulations relating to improper influence. That didn't dispose me to give Michiko the satisfaction of hearing me say so. Nor did the smug smile on her face. I'd come to tolerate and even appreciate the precise, pedantic side of Hara's character, but the idea of the pair of them nit-picking their way through the rule book and coming up with this feeble justification of his behaviour struck me as being contemptible, and made me furious.

"I see. Very ingenious. And no doubt Hara's cooked up some equally glib and specious excuse for deceiving his wife."

Well, that did it. Michiko whirled round in her seat, her eyes glittering with rage, and practically hissed at me while struggling to find words. "How *dare* you!" was all she finally managed. Ugly red streaks had appeared at either side of her neck, and a few seconds later she bolted to her feet and took herself off without another word, leaving me feeling as stupid and inept as I was angry.

Chapter 9

By THE TIME I ROUNDED THE LAST CORNER AND COULD SEE my house not far ahead, I felt exhausted and ached all over. In simple physical terms that was only to be expected: it had after all been much the longest walk I'd achieved since being shot. Quite apart from that, however, I felt shattered after the conversation with Michiko and its explosive climax, and was hardly calmer than when she had stormed off. My mind was in a turmoil and though I tried to order my thoughts I couldn't seem to engage the right gear.

Basically, I realised that I was still furious with Michiko and Hara, and that until I could come to terms with my anger I wouldn't be able to think straight. It was so humiliating to think that they had been discussing me, quite possibly while lying in bed together in some love hotel after enjoying themselves. Patronisingly giving some thought to what they no doubt saw as a purely technical problem for which a rational solution could be found.

It was something to have finally brought my worries over my sister-in-law's affair with Hara into the open and no longer have to pussyfoot around the subject. Moreover, Michiko hadn't flown off the handle initially. She had gone some way to understanding my point of view, and even suggested a possible way out of my dilemma. One which was as unappealing to me as it was ingenious, but quite likely all the same to faze any bureaucrat in Tokyo who might at some point be given the job of initiating disciplinary action against me.

All the same, I couldn't stop fuming over the whole thing. Michiko and Hara had insulted me, and whatever rationalisation they'd worked out between them to justify themselves, I still felt that Hara at least was behaving in a wretchedly shabby fashion. On the other hand I had made a fool of myself by saying so to Michiko. Was I right, anyway? How can an outsider possibly know enough to make judgements about somebody else's marriage? I seemed to have been stupidly insensitive to what I'd been doing to my own for a rather long time, after all.

I knew next to nothing about the personal lives of the Haras. I'd once glimpsed Mrs. Hara from a distance but had never met her, and I had no idea what the state of their marriage had been before her husband fell for Michiko more or less the moment he met her at the international summer school last year.

If asked to consider the bare facts, most people would probably make the same reasonable assumptions as I had. So I tried to reassure myself; but I couldn't get rid of the nagging fear that I might well be jumping to unjustifiable conclusions. What I thought was neither here nor there, anyway. Hara's domestic affairs were quite certainly none of my business, and I'd had no right to sound off at Michiko. However offended I was by her own remarks, perhaps I owed my sister-in-law at least a perfunctory apology.

Quite how and when I'd have a chance to offer it in person was another matter entirely. I took it for granted that she would have telephoned Hanae, given her version of what had passed between us, and cried off joining us for lunch. I didn't feel like meeting Michiko again or talking to her for a very long time, and couldn't imagine that her state of mind was much different from mine.

It's been my experience, on too many occasions to remember, that the surer I am of something, the more likely I am shortly to be proved wrong. Just as I was a few seconds later, when I arrived home. Heaving a sigh, I opened the sliding front door and called out the conventional, "I'm back!"

My continuing sense of outrage was by then tinged with sheepishness, and at the same time I experienced a sinking feeling, quite expecting a return to the pre-shooting coldness between Hanae and me. So what ought to have been a cheery shout was more of a mutter, actually. Quite audible nevertheless, because sure enough there was Hanae standing there on the wooden step beyond the little entryway, looming over me like a figure of doom. Worse, through the open screen door leading to the general purpose downstairs room I could see Michiko, scrubbing furiously with a paper tissue at a face stained with tears.

She looked as wretched as I felt, and I reacted impulsively. I kicked off my shoes, pushed past Hanae without another word and went directly inside to Michiko, who was kneeling on one of the plump, silk-covered floor cushions, a glass of what looked like whisky on a lacquer tray beside her. Then, although the manoeuvre sent agonising pains shooting through my back, I got down on my knees too, bowed as low as I could before her and swallowed my injured pride.

"What I said was crass, but nevertheless I ask your pardon. I am sincerely sorry."

I've never understood why so many people find it difficult to the point of impossibility to apologise for anything, even when they have good reason to. Believe me, I know what I'm talking about. We Japanese police officers are given a lot of discretion in dealing with offenders. Particularly in cases of technical infringements of the law when there's been no actual injury or other harm done. Speeding, for example, or not being able to produce a valid driving licence. We generally let the culprits off. Not exactly scot-free, mind you. We deliberately put them to a certain

60

amount of inconvenience, make them hang about in a police station for a couple of hours and answer a lot of irrelevant questions, that sort of thing. Just to drive it home to them that they're in the wrong, and make them think twice about doing the same thing again.

The final stage in that particular time-honoured ritual is when the offender is made to sit there like a naughty schoolchild and write out a letter expressing contrition and a determination to respect the law in future. It's remarkable how many people wriggle and squirm and try to get out of doing it, even to the extent of offering money or favours in lieu.

Resident foreigners, Westerners in particular, are the worst of the lot. They're forever forgetting to renew their alien registration on time or neglecting to carry identification, and the business of apologising in writing really upsets them. We've had people beg *not* to be let off; to be allowed to pay the hefty fine prescribed by the penal code instead. Anything to avoid saying they're sorry, even insincerely. And they say we Orientals are the ones who can't bear to lose face! Speaking personally, when I have egg on mine and know it's wholly or mainly my own fault I'm generally willing to admit it. I don't enjoy doing so, but it's better than feeling soiled.

A cynic might point out another reason one should apologise when conscious of being in the wrong. It disarms. I don't necessarily expect to be believed when I claim that in my own case that isn't the primary reason for my doing it; but all the same it's a bonus worth having.

My apology to Michiko that Sunday lunchtime was followed by silence for several seconds. Then she reached out a hand and rested it for a moment on my forearm: the second time she had touched me that day. Whatever her affair with Hara had or hadn't done to her emotions, it had certainly made Michiko physically demonstrative.

"It's all right," she said, and sniffed. "I don't really blame you."

61

That seemed to surprise Hanae, who had followed me into the room and now came over to me.

"I'll help you get up," she said, offering me her hand. "You can't be doing your back much good down there." Her manner wasn't exactly affectionate, but she expressed concern for me and that was a relief. I was glad of her help, too, in getting into a more comfortable position, sitting on the tatami matting against the wall, my legs stretched out and a cushion behind my sore back.

Without consciously trying to, I'd done something right, in the sense that my apology seemed to have satisfied Michiko, mollified Hanae and cleared the air generally. It also helped Michiko to pull herself together. She managed a rueful little smile as she got up. "I must look a sight," she said, and headed for the bathroom. After she'd gone Hanae and I looked at one another.

"I meant it," I said. "I'd no right to come out with such a hurtful remark. It's just that I've had to bottle up my feelings about all this for so long, and what with one thing and another . . ."

Hanae's stiff expression had softened. "I think I understand. We should have talked about it between ourselves properly. Instead of hiding behind all those hints and evasions."

I tried to shrug, and immediately thought better of it. "Well, I'm grateful to Michiko for forgiving me. But the problem doesn't seem likely to go away, does it?"

Another silence, but a companionable one this time, broken by the ringing of the phone in the kitchen. "I'll get it," Hanae said, but she hadn't reached the *fusuma* screen door when the ringing stopped. There's no such thing as soundproofing in a traditional Japanese house, and we could hear what Michiko said from the moment she picked up the receiver.

"Hello? Yes, this is the Otani house . . . one moment, I'll fetch him . . . who . . . *Takeshi*, is that you? Yes, of course it's me . . . oh, all right, I suppose . . . no, no, I'll tell you later. Ring me at home this evening. Yes, me too . . . hang on."

I had hauled myself to my feet again by the time Michiko slid the door open and reappeared, saying, "You're wanted urgently, It's—"

"Hara. Yes. Thank you." I went to the phone, and Michiko closed the door behind me. A thoughtful gesture, but conscious that the two women could hear me as clearly as Hanae and I had heard Michiko talking, I tried to sound calm and businesslike when I spoke.

"Otani here. Good afternoon."

"I'm sorry to disturb you at home, sir."

"That's all right. What's on your mind?"

"I've just had a call from the headquarters' duty officer. I'm at home myself—just about to leave—so I don't have much detail yet. But I thought you ought to know at once that we have a report of a murder."

"Oh? Anybody we know?"

"Well, yes, sir. That's why I thought you might like me to send a car for you. According to the report, the dead man is Hideki Suminoe."

Chapter 10

THE BODY HAD BEEN DISCOVERED AT ASHIYA, LESS THAN FIF-
teen minutes by car from Rokko in light Sunday traffic; and
since Hara had them send a car for me right away, I arrived
at the scene shortly before he did himself. On the way I'd
done my best to remember the details of the telephone conversation in which I'd pumped my Rotarian friend Fumio
Iwai about Hideki Suminoe. So I wasn't altogether unprepared for the grandeur of the house to which I was driven.

The price of land in the cities and suburbs of Japan being
what it is, the homes of even the very rich don't run to
extensive grounds. Nevertheless, the Suminoe residence
occupied a sizeable plot quite big enough to have accom-
modated three or four modern detached houses or a fair-
sized apartment block. The fact that it didn't suggested to
me that in spite of Iwai's suggestion that, as he had put it,
Suminoe hadn't always had "money to chuck about," he
couldn't be all that much of a self-made man. That plot
could never have survived the lean postwar years intact unless the family had always been well-heeled.

There wasn't a lot to be seen from the road: just a long
wall about a metre and a half high, built of massive, perfectly graded stone blocks. That alone must have cost a

packet. The stonework had a graceful inward curve as if the original idea had been to construct a traditional Japanese castle donjon, but was abandoned after phase one. For the stonework was topped by a handsome plaster wall about as high again, and finished with dull grey ceramic tiles.

The mixture of styles was disconcerting, and out of place in a narrow street in what was otherwise an ordinary if expensive residential area. Had it been possible to view it from a reasonable distance, the exterior of the property might have looked impressive and dignified, a little like a Buddhist temple perhaps. Even mellowed by the last of the sunlight of a winter afternoon, to me it seemed to verge on the vulgarly ostentatious, the sort of thing gangster barons sometimes commission for themselves.

The main gate, shut and surmounted by a closed-circuit video camera, certainly suggested that it had been supplied to the order of a wary and suspicious home-owner. It was a formidable metal affair mounted on tracks, and looked as if it would stop a tank. Clearly it was mechanically operated. To one side of it was a conventional, raised wooden wicket gate big enough to admit one person at a time. This stood open but was guarded by a uniformed patrolman who made such a show of saluting that he must have been warned of the imminent arrival of big shots from prefectural headquarters.

Since my back had taken quite a lot of punishment one way and another already that day, I took my time over easing myself out of the back of the police car, and had just completed the process when a second patrol vehicle pulled up. Hara emerged from it and approached me, all earnest officiousness. I'd hardly expected him to show up in jeans and trainers, but was a little surprised to note that his choice of clothes made no concession to the fact that it was a Sunday.

"I'm sorry not to have been here to receive you, sir."

"You had further to come than I did," I pointed out rather tersely after first acknowledging the still doggedly saluting patrolman. I might have made my peace after a fashion with Michiko, but I wasn't feeling any more amiable towards her lover. "Well, are we going to have that gate opened and get one of these cars inside out of sight, or what? We certainly don't need two blocking the road."

Hara, at his most bland, paid no attention to my tetchy manner. "I gather that an assistant inspector from the local divisional station's in charge here at present. With your permission I'll go in and consult him."

I've already mentioned that he's a bulky fellow, and for some reason the sight of him high-stepping delicately through the narrow wicket gate amused me and made me feel a little better. Anyway, having no intention of concerning myself further with transport and parking arrangements, I followed and was able to see the house itself for the first time.

It stood well back from the outer wall. The area inside the main gate was gravelled, and led directly to a detached double garage with what looked like living accommodation above. The garage doors were of the up-and-over type and were raised, revealing the glossy hood of a big black executive-style Nissan dwarfing the grey Honda Civic parked beside it.

The house itself was to one side. It was built in the smug western style now popular with the sort of architects that wealthy private clients patronise; and boasted amply proportioned windows, two on either side of the panelled front door and five on the floor above. Most of the space in front was also covered with fine white gravel, but on this side it was raked in a wave effect round a large, irregular island hillock of soft green moss, in which were embedded two enormous natural boulders. They were beautifully shaped and wonderfully weathered, with patches of lichen growing on them. It was in fact a perfect Zen garden, but in completely the wrong setting.

I would have liked to stand and look at those great stones on their cushion of jade-green moss for a long time, but it seemed that no sooner had Hara gone into the house through the front door than he reappeared, followed by a

66

uniformed assistant inspector, whose face I recognised and whose name I ought to have known but couldn't for the life of me recall. Not that it mattered, because Hara did the honours as the young man saluted.

"This is Assistant Inspector Chiba, sir."

"Ah, yes, of course. Good afternoon, Mr. Chiba. Perhaps you'd put me in the picture briefly, before I go inside."

"Sir. As divisional duty officer, approximately forty-five minutes ago I received a telephone message from the senior patrolman assigned to the police box located some three hundred metres from here. He stated that one of the two servants resident at this house had run to the box in evident distress, to report a death and an attempted suicide—"

"You didn't mention a suicide," I snapped at Hara. "Go on, Mr. Chiba."

Chiba looked a bit uncomfortable as he took up his story again. "Yes, sir. Um, having bicycled here himself to investigate, the senior patrolman decided he needed immediate specialist support, and as I explained, rang me. I arrived here within a few minutes, agreed that it seemed clear a serious crime had been committed, and accordingly contacted prefectural headquarters at once."

"I see. And now you have specialist support in the person of Inspector Hara here. Not to mention myself getting in the way. What can we expect to find inside?"

"Sir, the body of an elderly gentleman identified as Hideki Suminoe, the owner of the house. I . . ." he swallowed twice before continuing. "I satisfied myself that he was beyond medical help before doing anything else. The two servants are also inside: Yasuo Iida says he is employed as driver and general handyman, and his wife Emiko is cook and housekeeper. It was Mrs. Iida who ran to the police box to raise the alarm. While her husband remained with Mr. Toshio Suminoe, who is, I understand, the dead man's nephew."

"He's the attempted suicide, I presume. Does *he* need medical attention?"

"Not according to him, sir. By the time the officer from

the police box arrived he was conscious and insisting he was all right. I've spoken to him myself and he certainly seems to be, but no doubt the police medical examiner will be willing to take a look at him when he arrives to certify the death."

"On his way, is he, Hara?"

"He has been summoned." Hara sounded stiff and offended, probably because I hadn't let him get a word in edgewise; and turned to Chiba. "What had this Toshio Suminoe been up to?"

"I haven't presumed to question him beyond asking him how he felt, sir. But according to the Iidas, they were in their quarters above the garage watching television, and during a quiet moment Mrs. Iida thought she could hear a car engine below. They had a bit of an argument about it before Iida went to check. His wife was right. He found Suminoe sitting in the Nissan with the engine running and the garage doors closed—"

"How had he got in without being heard, then?"

Chiba turned to me with apparent reluctance. I suppose he felt less intimidated talking to Hara. "There's a side door, sir. Anyway, Iida says he immediately opened up the main doors, but he has yet to make a statement about what happened after that. That's all I can report at this stage, sir."

I thought I owed the young man a pat on the back. "Right, that's very clear, Mr. Chiba. Quite right not to guess at what you don't know. Time we went inside, Inspector, don't you think?"

Hara nodded. "I do. The doctor and the scenes-of-crime team should be here any minute."

Time was when it was routine to take off one's shoes and put on slippers when going inside even quite big western-style public buildings. The tradition lives on in a good many schools and a few universities, but these days most of us are quite used to keeping our shoes on from morning to night. It still gives me a jolt to go into a private house in outdoor footwear, though, and I hesitated at the Suminoe

68

front door. Once over the threshold, however, I had other things to occupy my mind.

Chiba had gone ahead into a spacious lobby, and hovered outside the open door of a large room furnished as a library or study. At first glance inside I could see a middle-aged couple sitting stiffly and well forward side by side on a sofa; and a pair of legs protruding from an armchair. Between the sofa and the legs—their owner was wearing jeans, thick, crumpled white socks and those wretched trainer things—stood a bare-headed patrolman, keeping an eye on things.

Chiba looked at me enquiringly. "Would the Superintendent wish to, er . . .?" he murmured discreetly, for all the world like a salesman in an expensive menswear shop.

"Later. Take us through to, er . . ." His style was infectious, I thought, as he nodded and moved on. I supposed the kitchen regions must be ahead, but Chiba led us to and through an elegantly furnished, carpeted living room with a formidable array of control panels, loudspeakers and screens occupying most of one wall. A Yamaha grand piano softened the effect: its keyboard was exposed, the lid was raised a few inches, and several printed scores and loose sheets jostled for space on the music stand. Beyond the living room was a small, glassed-in conservatory leading to a short, covered walkway, and at the end of *that* the entrance to a single-storey Japanese-style annexe which had been invisible from outside the front of the house.

This was much more like it. Modern fire regulations prohibit new rice-straw thatch-roofed constructions, but Suminoe had paid for the expensive alternative: layers of laminated birch-strips such as you find at Buddhist temples and Shinto shrines. From outside the annexe didn't look all that large, but it was handsome, and the view of the interior through the open sliding door was something else again. For the "notorious" Noh fanatic Suminoe hadn't gone to the extreme of having his own stage installed, but he'd come close.

At the far end of what was otherwise a single, harmoniously proportioned space were two screen doors behind which were presumably a dressing and a wardrobe room. The floor of the main area was covered with fragrant tatami mats of the palest greenish-gold, except for a square in the centre. This measured about two metres each way and was of highly polished dark wood, flush with the surrounding mats.

A narrow wooden walkway linked the back of this "stage" to the left-hand sliding door, and I realised that it must be an improvised "flower path": the bridge along which the principal performers make their gliding entrances in real Noh theatres. This didn't occur to me until later, because my immediate attention was focused on the crumpled heap in the middle of the "stage."

In life, Hideki Suminoe had looked to me like a pompous, impatient, self-important man. In death, and in full costume and wearing the painted wooden mask of the classic Old Man character of the Noh drama, he looked awe-inspiring.

Chapter 11

THE RICHLY EMBROIDERED SILK BROCADE USED TO MAKE NOH costumes is so stiff and heavy, and the robes themselves so voluminous, that what was lying there about four metres from where we stood didn't look much like a human body. As a matter of fact, the only visible flesh was that of one hand, the fingers curled but not clenched, looking soft and vulnerable against the glossy dark wood of the central performance area. I could also see one foot, but that was enclosed in a snow-white *tabi* sock of the type that women wear with formal kimonos. Women, and Noh principals, of course. The painted wooden mask with its wispy pretend beard concealed the face completely, so had it not been for the hand, the utterly still figure might have been a grotesque, life-sized puppet flung down by its manipulator.

Hara made to step forward, but I grabbed him by the sleeve to stop him and turned to Assistant Inspector Chiba. "You've been inside and touched him?"

He looked queasy as he nodded. "I had to, sir. He might have been alive."

"Yes, yes, of course. Anybody else, though?"

"Iida the handyman, maybe. Probably not his wife. Oh,

71

and the senior patrolman from the police box told me he felt the wrist for a pulse before reporting in."

"Quite enough for the moment. Hara, you and I can wait till the doctor and your specialists have done their jobs before we go blundering about in there. What made you so sure it wasn't a natural death, Mr. Chiba?"

"Sir, he has a cord wound so tightly round his neck that it's embedded in the skin."

"Mightn't it have been suicide?"

"No. It's tied with a bow. I don't see how he could possibly have done that to himself."

"Well, that remains to be confirmed, but you were obviously right to decide that something very weird has been going on in this house."

I could sense that Hara was smouldering with resentment over the way I was taking the lead, but that was just too bad. He could perfectly well have gone to the house at once and taken a look round before ringing to suggest that I should join him. If he had, he could have established his authority at the scene before I arrived.

Indeed I wondered why he hadn't, and it struck me that he might not be altogether convinced that all his bland plotting and scheming with Michiko to find a way to negate my official concern over their affair had been so clever after all. If I was right, it could be that he wanted to show me what a good boy he was about keeping me completely in the picture so far as his work was concerned. In which case I wasn't averse to showing him who was boss.

"Stay where you are, both of you." It came out with satisfying peremptoriness, and the two of them stood there while I slipped my feet out of my shoes and stepped up the inch or so from outside the sliding door and on to the chilly, slightly yielding surface of the tatami. Japanese forensic scientists have had to devise some techniques that I can hardly believe are needed in the west, and nowadays it's even possible for experts to lift prints made by stockinged feet on these rice-straw mats with their coverings of finely woven grass.

So I kept well clear of the body, by side-stepping through the door and taking just two diagonal paces that put me well inside the annexe but not much nearer to the wooden stage area. From there I could, however, get a much better impression of the whole interior of the late Hideki Suminoe's personal playground. It confirmed my first thought that very high-quality materials had been used in its construction. Nevertheless, I felt there was something fundamentally wrong about the concept of a private Noh theatre-that-wasn't, and it was distasteful to think of Suminoe posturing there alone in his costly finery.

Then I turned round and caught sight of the wall behind me. I must admit that I couldn't repress a shudder, because for one crazy instant I saw a second stage, and another crumpled, discarded puppet. It was, of course, the image reflected in a vast mirrored panel that took up much of the wall space at the side of the doorway outside which Hara and Chiba were obediently awaiting my pleasure.

"This must have given you a jolt," I said to Chiba, since I couldn't very well pretend that the reflection hadn't startled me. "What an extraordinarily vain man he must have been. I've only seen a mirror this size in a love hotel before."

"They also have them in practice rooms for ballet dancers, and with good reason," Hara said, having leant forward, craned his neck and taken a peep for himself. He sounded haughty and censorious as well as miffed. "If I may say so, the placing of a mirror so that he could watch himself rehearsing might be evidence of an inclination to self-criticism in a serious amateur as much as vanity."

Stung, I reminded him tartly that it was he who in first telling me about Suminoe had made a point of mentioning what a show-off he was, and then harrumphed myself to a full stop when I noticed that young Chiba was obviously drinking in the spectacle of two senior officers swapping asperities. Hara also pulled himself together, seeming to realise that he'd come close to impertinence, and when he addressed me again it was with proper courtesy.

"May I suggest, sir, that the Assistant Inspector might be spared to go and supervise his men? It would obviously be desirable for the main gate to be opened in readiness for the arrival of the scenes-of-crime team with their van. And the doctor."

"You're right. Yes, please do that, Chiba. There's no point in our standing around here any longer, either." I backed out of the annexe along the same line I'd gone in, bent painfully and wiggled my feet back into my shoes with the aid of the little shoe-horn I always carry in my jacket pocket. Then, Chiba having taken himself off with evident reluctance, I turned to Hara.

"Well, Inspector. Until we hear what the doctor has to say I'm not quite so ready to use the word murder as that young man is. Assuming he's right, though, I presume you'll take charge of the investigation into this affair yourself rather than delegating it?"

I spoke in a brisk, official sort of way, and rather expected Hara to respond accordingly, even though there was no longer a witness to our conversation. In fact he looked at me with a sad expression on his moon face and shook his head slowly from side to side before heaving an exasperated sigh and replying in plain, unvarnished man-to-man language.

"Look, this can't go on. You can have my resignation in the morning."

It shook me, I can tell you; and not least because I could see he meant it. I thought hard and fast.

"I agree the situation between us has to be sorted out, but talk of resignation's ridiculous. If I'd seen you as nothing but an embarrassment after you got involved with my wife's sister I'd have pulled strings at the Agency and had you transferred to another force whether you liked it or not, and without the slightest compunction. It would have been the easiest thing in the world to arrange."

He nodded with a little grimace, then sucked in a big breath. "But you didn't. Mind if I ask why not?"

"Because I don't want to lose you, confound it! But this

74

isn't the time or place to argue the matter. You've a job to do."

"Thanks for reminding me. I'd never have guessed," he said, very bitterly, but then his face changed. "I'm sorry. Thank you for what you just said. I'd like to go on being your head of criminal investigation, and try to justify your confidence in me. But I can't cope if you're going to needle me every chance you get, snipe at me in front of a junior officer and generally throw your weight about."

I lost my temper completely and shouted at Hara then: the first time I'd done such a thing to a subordinate for many years. I yelled that he was behaving in an astonishing, unforgivably insubordinate manner. That he might have a high opinion of himself because he was a fast-stream graduate inspector in his thirties, but that to me he was an insolent, unsufferably conceited jackass. Then I reminded him at the top my voice that he was talking to a three-star superintendent who was not only old enough to be his father but was also his commander and reporting officer. People in the street must have been able to hear me: goodness knows what young Chiba and the little group gathered in the study thought was going on.

When I eventually ran out of breath and just stood there glaring at him Hara was very red in the face and the muscles of his mouth worked, but he seemed to be bereft of speech. The silence lasted a long time until at last he put his arms straight down by his sides and inclined his head in submission.

"I humbly beg your pardon, Commander," he said in a strangled voice, and it must have nearly killed him.

All the same, his apology was just as effective with me as mine had earlier been with his mistress, and my own fury abated. So I temporised.

"I'm not overlooking the tone you've presumed to take with me, but in the light of that apology we'll set it on one side just for the present. And you might as well go on speaking frankly. Answer one question. Why did you ask me to come here this afternoon? You didn't have to."

Hara's high colour was fading but he still looked thoroughly chastened.

"No, sir, I know I didn't. I asked you because the moment I heard the name Suminoe I thought—as I venture to suggest you now think—that this case is going to turn out to be unusually interesting. And I believe that if I'm going to crack it I shall need your help."

"Help?" I rather boomed the word. In spite of having humbled himself, Hara still didn't seem to have grasped my point. On the contrary, he looked straight at, and there was a hint of defiance in his eyes.

"Help, sir. Let's be clear about that. You can overrule me if you choose to, obviously, and if you do I shall accept your decision without question. However, as long as I'm in charge of the investigation I want to call the shots."

"Do you indeed?"

"Yes, Commander, I do. You realise that this Toshio Suminoe who is alleged to have tried to kill himself is the man who saw you being shot in Kobe?"

"The possibility had occurred to me."

"Of course it has. I've already told you how much I respect your reputation as a detective."

He had, and it had embarrassed me. "So?"

"So I want to take it from here, please. With your expert advice, if you'll give it."

I thought about this. I had calmed down and had to admire his spirit, but I was still seriously displeased with Hara. Heads of prefectural police forces aren't supposed to rush about doing the work of their subordinates for them, but if I'd been physically fit and free from domestic tensions I think I might well have been pig-headed enough to take personal charge anyway. It had already been a peculiarly demanding day, however, and I knew in my heart of hearts that what Hara proposed was sensible.

"Very well," I said grudgingly. "It's all yours, and you're welcome to my advice when you choose to seek it." We stared at each other for a long moment. Then Hara not only inclined his head but bowed, which made me feel better.

"Thank you, sir."

"Good luck. And, Hara, try to find a happy mean between talking officialese at me and being confoundedly rude, would you?"

He blinked a few times and then cracked a small smile. "I'll try, sir, yes."

"Do that. Now, is there anything you want of me now, or shall I go home and continue making peace with your lady friend?"

Hara blinked again, visibly deciding whether or not to go back to being offended. The truce held. "Could you stay long enough to sit in while I question Suminoe at least, and maybe the servants? I'd value your impressions of them while they're still in a state of nervous tension. I . . . ah, I think Michiko will keep for a while."

Chapter 12

I WAS EVENTUALLY DELIVERED BACK TO ROKKO ABOUT THREE hours after I'd left. Michiko had gone home, so I was spared any further ticklish negotiations with her. Hanae said that she and her sister had "talked things over," but didn't seem to be inclined to pass on any conclusions they might have arrived at. The two of them couldn't have eaten much, because there was plenty of chicken fricassee left for me, and Hanae put a potato in the microwave to go with it. I would have preferred noodles, but Hanae had recently become convinced—no doubt after reading an article in *Croissant*— that baked potatoes were highly nutritious, and it was hardly the moment for me to suggest that we'd been having them rather often.

In any case, I was so hungry that I didn't care all that much, and attacked with relish everything she put on the kitchen table in front of me. Hanae stood and watched me for a while, and then poured herself a cup of green tea, pulled out the other chair and sat down.

"Well, aren't you going to tell me about it?"

I'd had every intention of doing so anyway, and now that my demanding stomach had been appeased I embarked on an account of the way I'd spent my afternoon, omitting only my personal exchanges with Hara. Hanae listened intently to my description of the Suminoe house and extracted from me more details about it than I had been conscious of noticing at the time. She shuddered when I told her about the appearance of the body and the disconcerting mirror image, but I think that was more or less for form's sake. Hanae isn't altogether the tender plant she sometimes pretends to be.

Up to then I'd simply been describing what I'd seen, without theorising. Time was, years ago, when I hardly ever volunteered anything at all about a current investigation to Hanae, much less discussed it with her. Mind you, she'd always had ways and means of winkling a certain amount out of me, but it must have been hard work for her in those days. As I got older I took her into my confidence much more, and learned to trust absolutely in her discretion.

So that Sunday I went on to tell her about the interviews Hara had conducted at the opulent Suminoe house with me sitting in, while his specialist team swarmed all over the annexe. This, of course, after the doctor had examined the body of Hideki Suminoe and declared himself satisfied that the cause of death had been strangulation. He'd also taken a look at the nephew, Toshio Suminoe, and agreed that physically at least there was nothing much wrong with him.

Hara had begun with the Iidas, of course, and I thought it was fair enough for him to see them together. They must have been not only stressed and traumatised by what had happened so recently, but also prey to developing anxiety about their future, since it emerged at once that the flat above the garage was the only home they had. Yasuo Iida, a lean, stringy little man, was just turned fifty and his wife Emiko three years younger. She by contrast was plump, and must have been quite a looker as a young woman. They had a grown-up daughter married to a truck driver living up north in Iwate Prefecture, but hadn't bothered to keep in touch with her for years.

They said they'd been working for Suminoe for about eight and a half years. It must presumably have occurred to them from time to time during that period that their employer wasn't immortal, was getting on in years anyway, and that there was every prospect that they'd outlive him. However, they both seemed not so much shocked as astonished at the idea that Suminoe was actually dead. Nevertheless, they were far from stupid, and Mrs. Iida had quite as much to say for herself as her husband did. In fact, as they began to relax a little in response to Hara's sympathetic, courteous questioning they often contradicted each other. I found it easy to visualise them bickering in front of the television set, debating whether or not she could hear a car engine downstairs.

I say they contradicted each other, but it was only over trivialities. Hara said afterwards that he believed they were telling the truth, and with some reservations I agreed. At a later stage the couple could almost certainly be relied on to supply any amount of information about the late Suminoe's life-style, habits and associates. For immediate purposes, though, it was enough to have a full account of the day's events from the point of view of the Iidas.

Sunday was their weekly free day together. They each had an additional half day off during the week, but took it on different days, so Suminoe had one or the other of them around six days a week. He fended for himself on a Sunday, but Emiko Iida always left enough prepared food in the refrigerator for him unless he specifically told her not to bother. Noh performances often take place on Sundays, and for those actually taking part involve the best part of the whole day at the theatre. Didn't the old man require Iida's services as a driver on such occasions, Hara asked. Sometimes, it seemed, in which case Iida was always happy to take an alternative day off. The Iidas obviously weren't all that keen on each other's company.

Anyway, that particular day they were both off duty, and had wandered down to the local department store in the morning to buy a few odds and ends in the food hall for their own lunch and evening meal. Arriving back at the house at about eleven-thirty, they were just in time to see

Suminoe opening his front door to admit his nephew Toshio. Nothing unusual about that: Toshio and his elder brother Koichi were frequent weekend visitors.

The Iidas had their lunch, with the television already on I should imagine, and then settled down to a lazy afternoon. Until, as reported to us earlier, they started arguing the toss over whether or not Emiko could hear a car engine. In spite of the solemnity of the occasion she directed a self-satisfied smirk at me when her husband admitted to Hara that she'd been right. He, Yasuo, had heard it himself as he was going downstairs, and once he discovered that the main garage doors were closed he ran to the side door, only to find it locked from inside. So he had to go back upstairs and fetch his electronic keypad (another meaningful look from Emiko at this further evidence of her husband's general inadequacy) in order to open up the main doors.

Iida then took in the sight of the Nissan and a length of rubber hosepipe leading from the exhaust pipe to a barely open rear window. From then on he seems to have acted with commendable presence of mind. He told Hara he wrenched open the door, turned off the engine and took possession of the ignition keys. He then dragged the comatose young man out of the car and into the open air, where Suminoe almost at once began to stir, feebly protesting.

Needless to say, Emiko had by then come downstairs to see what was going on, and between them the Iidas carried the nephew into the main house and on to the sofa on which they were currently sitting. Wondering where his uncle could be, Iida went first upstairs to the old man's bedroom, and checked the other second-floor rooms before eventually reaching the annexe where he obviously got a far worse shock than any of the rest of us. We had, after all, been warned there was a body in there, if not that it was arrayed in gorgeous Noh costume.

Given the stomach-turning nature of his discovery, Iida did well to keep his head, and it was both sensible and understandable on his part to have sent his wife to fetch a policeman while he stayed with Toshio Suminoe, who couldn't necessarily be counted on to remain tractable. They could have used the telephone, but in Japanese cities one's never very far from a manned *koban* or police box, and most people instinctively turn to their local patrolman when in trouble.

Hara let the Iidas go back to their own quarters once the main outline of events was clear and they had both confirmed that after he came round, the nephew Suminoe remained mute. They'd each tried to persuade him to open up, but all he would say was that he didn't need a doctor. By the time they reported that to Hara, of course he *had* been examined, albeit perfunctorily, by the duty police doctor, who had ordered him to bed in a spare room upstairs but told us that in his view hospital treatment was quite unnecessary.

That was all very well, but, as I explained to Hanae, it didn't solve the problem of what was to be done with him. Here was an attempted suicide who on the face of things was also a prime murder suspect. I've made it abundantly clear that Inspector Hara is a stickler for the letter of the rule book, always at pains to base his judgements firmly on the evidence.

Nevertheless, as we made our way upstairs to see what young Mr. Suminoe could be persuaded to say for himself I was pretty confident that Hara was, like me, provisionally theorising that Toshio Suminoe had killed his uncle and then in a fit of remorse, or overcome by the horror of what he had done, tried to do away with himself.

It was a good enough working hypothesis, but one look at the young man lying on the bed upstairs and staring up unseeingly at the ceiling made me doubt if it could be sustained for long. My first impression was of a gentle and sensitive man with a personality likely to match his fine-drawn, attractively moulded features. He was fully conscious, and answered at once when Hara identified himself and asked him if his name was Toshio Suminoe. He went on to give his age as twenty-seven, and an address in the westernmost ward of Osaka, not very far away.

His voice was low and pleasantly modulated, and having been told how uncommunicative he had been earlier I was surprised by the ready way he responded to Hara's preliminary, fact-finding questions. I was even more surprised when he turned his head and spoke directly to me. "The Inspector didn't introduce you, but you're the gentleman who was hit by a bullet in Kobe around New Year, aren't you? The head of the prefectural police. I saw it happen, and gave the police a statement. And followed the reports in the papers, of course. I'm so glad you're up and about again."

His manner was politely interested, for all the world as though we were fellow guests at some social occasion. I muttered something suitably banal in reply, and Hara seemed to take the exchange as a signal to turn up the heat. No doubt he was thinking, as I was, that Toshio had overheard me savaging him, and wanted to assert himself.

"Yes, well, we're here to discuss your health, not the Superintendent's. Among other things. We have evidence that you attempted to commit suicide by inhaling car exhaust fumes in an enclosed space, and might well have succeeded in doing so had not the handyman Yasuo Iida intervened when he did."

Suminoe threw me a sweet little smile, as though apologising for having to break off our conversation, and then answered Hara.

"Well, I suppose there's not much point in my denying it, is there, then?"

"You admit that you tried to kill yourself?"

A little sigh, then, "Yes, at the time I did intend to."

"Why?"

"Surely I'm not obliged to give you my reasons, Inspector? Let's just say I'm tired of life."

"I see. What time did you arrive at this house today?"

"About noon, I think, or a bit earlier."

"What was the purpose of your visit?"

"My uncle asked me to call."

"Have you any idea why?"

"I assumed that he was going to give me another of his lectures about my philosophy of life and try yet again to talk me into joining his company, and so it turned out."

"Mr. Suminoe, you are aware of what has happened to your uncle, of course?" Hara was on safe ground in taking that line. Even if the young man hadn't killed his uncle he couldn't possibly have failed to realise that all the police officers who'd descended on the house while he was recovering in the study had more serious things on their minds than his failed suicide attempt.

"I know he's dead," he said, flatly.

"And did you become aware of this before, or after you became so tired of life yourself that you tried to commit suicide?"

Toshio Suminoe closed his eyes for a few seconds, then opened them again and answered Hara's question in a firm, businesslike voice. "After my uncle had explained the errors of my ways to me for about the hundredth time, he became more agreeable and invited me to hear him rehearse a particular speech. I soon realised that what he really wanted was for me to help him get into his robes. So I did that. Then he started rehearsing, and I did my best to look impressed. After about a quarter of an hour I excused myself to go to the toilet. I took my time, and smoked a cigarette in there. When I got back to the annexe I . . . found him lying there. I thought he'd taken ill, had a stroke or something, but then I . . . it was ghastly. My first thought was to go and fetch Iida, but then I realised that everyone would take it for granted that I'd done it, and . . ."

Chapter 13

THERE WASN'T MUCH MORE I COULD TELL HANAE THAT SUN-day, beyond informing her of the obvious: that Hara had decided with my full support to take Toshio Suminoe into custody. His assertion of innocence had impressed me more than it should have done given the flimsiness of his story, and I felt curiously reassured that at least for the time being he'd be where somebody could keep an eye on him and make sure he didn't make any further attempt to do himself harm. Nevertheless, he was, and seemed likely to remain, under grave suspicion of having murdered his uncle.

Having handed Hara the responsibility for the investigation I had in fairness to him to do my best to keep out of his way so that he could get on with all the work entailed. There would be plenty: locating the dead man's next of kin and arranging for them to be informed, organising a post mortem to leave no possible doubt about the cause of death, and, needless to say, questioning the Iidas and Toshio Suminoe again and in much greater depth in due course.

Naturally I went on thinking about the whole affair and the curious coincidence of the younger Suminoe's having been a witness when I was shot, and I mooned about the house restlessly for a long time. Eventually, however, the sheer exhaustion resulting from the tumultuous events of the day—including my angry personal confrontations with both Michiko and Hara—got to me. I went to bed very early and, perhaps surprisingly in the circumstances, slept like a log.

The following morning I had other things to occupy my mind. I went into headquarters again, had a look at the daily information board and took it into my head to go along with the head of the traffic control division and the officer commanding our detachment of riot police to a meeting at the city hall chaired by the mayor of Kobe, to discuss the touchy subject of the forthcoming annual conference of the All-Japan Teachers' Union. This regular event, that sounds to an outsider as if it ought to be stupendously boring, has for many years been a headache to the authorities of whatever city it was allowed to be held in.

I used that word "allowed" advisedly. Nobody in charge of accepting bookings for the use of suitable halls ever wants the teachers on his premises. This is because the one thing you can count on is that wherever members of their union assemble, the thugs of the extreme right wing will appear in the vicinity with their beflagged and slogan-bedecked armoured trucks and their hideously noisy loudspeakers blaring out insults and tape recordings of "patriotic" songs.

Exercising their right to free speech, they call it, but it's intimidation pure and simple, of course. The trouble is that even just the threat of it's often effective. As soon as the rightists find out where the union plans to hold its conference, they get at and all too often succeed in "persuading" the management of the conference centre concerned—even if it's a local authority—to refuse or cancel the booking.

It's a fuss about nothing nowadays, a hangover from the fifties and sixties when the teachers' union was in fact dominated by pretty fiery left-wingers. There was nothing odd about that: Marxism was the orthodoxy of the Japanese intelligentsia during those years. So the teachers used indeed to make strident noises, even though the union was for all practical purposes powerless and had been since as far back as 1947, when General MacArthur with a stroke of the pen banned a planned national strike of all public servants. I well remember the sense of anticlimax when the teachers and their allies meekly climbed down. From a political point of view, their trade unions have been a bit of a joke ever since then.

To listen to the "patriots" ranting away, though, you'd think that instead of being a rather pathetic little rump organisation led nowadays by thoroughly respectable moderates, the All-Japan Teachers' Union is a sinister conspiracy of subversive communists still out to overthrow the government and get rid of the Emperor.

Full of what they pretend is righteous indignation, the bully-boys pursue and harass the poor old teachers relentlessly, and do their best to interfere with their meetings. And that year it was our turn to try to see fair play, because the annual conference was shortly to be held at a public hall in Kobe. The rightists tried to have the booking cancelled, but for once the union got the better of them by securing a legal ruling in their favor. They were guaranteed the use of the hall for their perfectly legitimate proceedings, and their enemies couldn't be permitted to wreck them.

There was a good deal of hand-wringing at the meeting at the city hall, and nothing much was agreed except that for the relevant two or three days all those involved in keeping the peace would have their hands full. However, my two tough, seasoned colleagues, while fully aware that they were in for a noisy and tiresome time, were confident that their men would be able to keep the two sides apart. Indeed the riot squad commander was, I suspect, rather looking forward to the chance to provide some vigorous practical exercise for his personnel, who when not training spend most of their working lives sitting about in grey buses with wire netting over the windows, reading magazines.

All three of us policemen knew that it would be necessary to keep a sharp eye open for any attempt to turn what

87

was generally an essentially ritual demonstration into a really dangerous *mêlée*, but it seemed unlikely to us at that stage that anybody would be seriously hurt. I was to remember our rashly complacent assumption only too bitterly in due course.

My muscles were aching as a result of my exertions of the previous day, but I nevertheless forced myself to take a lunchtime stroll on the way back to headquarters, where I found a message from Hara, asking if I could spare him half an hour some time in the afternoon. I was quite surprised to infer that he could spare *me* that much time when he ought to have been rushed off his feet; and said as much when, after I'd had a message passed to him to the effect that I was back, he came up to see me.

"The investigation is proceeding, I assure you, sir," he said coolly. "Several officers are following up various lines of enquiry, and a good deal of useful information has been assembled."

Unsurprisingly, we were both still touchy after the explosion of the previous day; and it was Hara who went on to make the atmosphere somewhat more relaxed. He took off his glasses and rubbed his eyes, then coughed and smiled briefly as he put them on again. "I'm sorry. I'm talking officialese again. Before I let you know how we're getting on, will you please accept my renewed and sincere apologies for the way I spoke to you yesterday?"

"In the circumstances, yes. We were both on edge, and I probably provoked you. I'm sorry if I did. We'll have to have a serious personal talk before long, but it'll do no harm to wait a while. So. Come and sit down. What's the state of play? How's your number one suspect?"

"Toshio Suminoe's physically all right. He seems to be in a state of complete emotional lassitude, but he's talking freely enough."

"Still protesting his innocence?"

"Yes. When I say he's talking, I mean just factually about himself and his uncle. He accepts that he's giving us

88

what sounds like a very tall story, but won't even speculate about who might have killed the old man if he didn't."

I winced inwardly at his reference to somebody not all that many years my senior as an old man, but let it pass. To Hara I too must have seemed well past my sell-by date. "I gather that—assuming for the sake of argument that he really is innocent—you think he might have an idea all the same?"

"Well, no. I'm inclined to think it points to his own guilt. If he could point the finger at anybody else, no matter who, surely he would, to extricate himself from the mess he's in."

"Time will tell, no doubt. Go on, and I'll try not to interrupt." Hara looked as if he had his doubts about that, and with good reason, but in fact I did hold my tongue for some time after he continued.

"What Toshio Suminoe did tell us is that his uncle never married, and that his own father died when he and his elder brother were boys. To his knowledge the only other living blood relative is his aunt Yoshiko, Hideki Suminoe's younger sister, who is the designated next of kin. She's a doctor, a partner in a fair-sized gynaecological and obstetric practice with its own maternity clinic in Himeji. It's useful in a way that it's in our prefecture, so we haven't had to involve any other force. I sent Junko Migishima, with a male detective from the Himeji division, to break the news to Dr. Yoshiko Suminoe yesterday evening, and she turned in a useful report this morning."

I wouldn't have expected any other kind of report from Junko, a very bright young woman indeed, and tried to make myself more comfortable in my chair, ready to pay attention.

"I've brought a photocopy for you to read at leisure, but if I may I'll summarise it briefly right away." I nodded at once. "She describes Dr. Suminoe as a well-dressed, alert woman who reacted to the news of her brother's death with obvious but well-controlled distress.

Needless to say, Junko-san could say no more about the circumstances than that they were such that there'd be a post mortem. Again the lady's response was what might be expected of a thoughtful, intelligent professional person, and although a doctor she made no attempt to press for more information. Not that Junko-san had any more at that stage to divulge anyway, of course. Dr. Yoshiko Suminoe gave her age as fifty-eight, and agreed that so far as she knew she was Hideki Suminoe's next of kin." Hara took off his glasses and rubbed his eyes again before resuming. He looked tired but fully in command of himself.

"She said she hadn't had much to do with her brother personally for many years, the last significant occasion being some fourteen or fifteen years earlier when the other brother died. His widow was adequately provided for and well able to bring up the two boys, but Uncle Hideki in effect appointed himself a kind of guardian and took a close interest in their progress from that time on. He also reminded his sister Yoshiko that she was his own next of kin, and that in the event of his own death he would expect her to look after the boys in his stead."

"I wonder what their mother thought of that," I mused aloud. "Is she still around?"

"Yes, and I'll be sending Junko Migishima to have a chat with her today or tomorrow. Toshio Suminoe still lives with his mother at the old family home. The school he teaches at is quite near. So far as the school principal knows Suminoe's on sick leave, by the way. I thought it might be helpful to get our own medical adviser to provide a certificate. Toshio's elder brother Koichi's married and has his own place, in Nishinomiya, which is worth bearing in mind isn't far from Ashiya and the scene of the murder. All this information is being checked, needless to say."

Hara paused, and when he spoke again his voice sounded livelier. "You'll see from the report that Dr. Yoshiko

Suminoe mentioned something else, of some interest. According to her, about five years ago Hideki Suminoe made a secret will."

Chapter 14

A SECRET WILL! IT SOUNDED DISTINCTLY INTRIGUING TO ME, but after delivering himself of that titbit in a meaningful sort of way Hara had merely gone on to say that he was getting in touch with the dead man's legal adviser. After which he took his leave, with no requests for advice but with a promise to keep me in the picture.

Left to myself, I tried to remember what I knew about wills in general. It didn't amount to much, even though in the early years of my police career I was required to study and to pass examinations in various aspects of the law. The emphasis, naturally, was on the penal code, but elements of the postwar civil code were also covered.

A legally competent Japanese adult could, I knew, make a valid will by writing the whole thing out personally, dating it and not only using a registered seal to authenticate it but also, unusually in Japan, writing his or her own name. Since credit cards became so fashionable we've had to get used to the idea of "signing" with a ballpoint pen instead of using the little personal seals most of us always carry, but when the civil code was drawn up it was an exceptional thing to do. Anyway, a will drawn up in that form was acceptable in law, and would generally be kept with other important family papers until needed.

Alternatively and more formally, a will can be dictated to a notary public in the presence of at least two witnesses, and signed and sealed by all present. I vaguely recalled that there are several other simplified methods that can be used in cases of emergency, but the details, if I ever knew them, had long since escaped me. The expression "secret will" conveyed nothing to me beyond the ordinary everyday meaning of those words, but Hara had spoken them as though they had some technical significance I'd be sure to grasp, and I wasn't about to admit my ignorance.

So I had recourse to the reference books in my outer office, and discovered that there's an authorised variation on the first of the two regular procedures I'd remembered, known as the holographic and the notarial methods of making a will. If a testator wants its contents to remain confidential until after his or her death, it's permissible for the holographic will to be signed and sealed in the presence of two people who haven't read it. They then watch the author insert the document into an envelope and seal it, and finally all present have to sign and seal the envelope to make it a legal "secret will."

In spite of all these sophisticated provisions in the civil code, so far as I knew very few Japanese bother to make wills. I couldn't think of anybody in my own family who ever had. Unless my private circumstances alter dramatically—if Hanae really were to leave and divorce me or die before me, for example—I expect to die intestate. No problem: the law as it stands provides automatically for widows, children and other close relatives.

Curious to know whether I was right in supposing that most people are equally casual, I made a couple of phone calls, to the family court secretariat and to the statistical bureau of the prefectural government. Within half an hour I had the confirmation I wanted. The population of Japan last year was just short of 123 million, and the annual death rate is currently about 6.5 a thousand.

93

With the aid of the old-fashioned abacus I keep rather furtively in a desk drawer since Kimura spotted it one day and reacted as if I was still living in the Stone Age, I worked out that about three quarters of a million—eight hundred thousand, to be more accurate—Japanese die in an average year. And do you know how many wills were probated in family courts throughout the country in the most recent year for which figures were available? Fewer than three thousand.

That did surprise me, I must admit, and though I don't know how it is in England, I expect it surprises you too, Mr. Melville. I'd been expecting to be given a total well into five figures. Anyway, I sat there for quite a while wondering how many of those three thousand wills had been of the secret variety. The family court registrar hadn't been able to tell me that, but I doubted very much if the total amounted to ten per cent. At most. In spite of the many radical changes in our society in the last few decades, we Japanese still tend to hold family conferences to decide important (not to mention a good many trivial) matters. Anybody wanting to make a special provision for disposing of assets without letting all concerned know would be regarded as being an oddball indeed.

I had just about reached that point in my reflections when the door was opened and Ninja Noguchi came in. He hadn't knocked, but then he never did. Probably because the weather had turned dull and chilly, he was unusually well dressed, though not to the degree that he'd smartened himself up to visit me in the hospital. He was wearing an almost respectable grey jacket and trousers, with one of those woollen sports shirts that button up to the neck. It was blue, and I caught a glimpse of a little crocodile emblem on the front. If he hadn't been so fat he'd have looked quite like one of the senior citizens you see in little parks, obediently doing undemanding physical jerks under the direction of some self-important group leader. There was a slightly conspiratorial look on his battered face, and it did my heart good to see him.

"Good afternoon, Ninja." I got up from my desk and went back to the low table at which I'd been sitting earlier with Hara.

"How you feeling?" he demanded as we settled into our usual places. "Had a busy day yesterday, I hear. Not overdoing it?"

"Been talking to Hara, have you?"

Noguchi made one of his characteristically economical gestures, but I knew him well enough to infer that he was well briefed on what had been going on during the past twenty-four hours. Knowing also that he was well acquainted with both the Haras and visited them from time to time—mainly to read bedtime stories to their little girl, I understand—it was a fairly safe bet that he knew something at least about Hara's complicated personal life. I'd had quite enough of that subject lately, so I stuck to business.

"Well, if you have you'll know that he's very much in charge of the Suminoe affair."

"Sure. Giving his orders, too. I just got back from talking to the Iida guy."

"The handyman. I saw him yesterday myself. Hara asked you to do that, did he? Did Iida's wife let him get a word in?"

Noguchi didn't exactly smile, but there was an air of self-satisfaction about him, which made sense as he gave me an account of the interview. He'd been warned in advance about Emiko Iida's strong personality and had therefore detached the husband by the simple expedient of asking Junko Migishima to interview the wife. Then he took Yasuo Iida for a walk and they ended up in a sushi bar. Good sushi washed down with plenty of *sake*'s very expensive and not really Ninja's style, but Iida had blossomed under the influence of such flattering treatment and become positively loquacious.

At least, according to Noguchi, who is himself taciturn to a degree, but none the less effective in conveying the salient points of his message. As I listened to him I mentally gave Hara full marks for asking him to quiz Iida, who

95

would have found him reassuringly casual and unvarnished. Ninja probably left the man with the impression that he'd been talking to a veteran plain-clothes patrolman rather than the most senior inspector at headquarters, and I found it easy to visualise the pair of them sitting up at a sushi bar getting on like a house on fire.

Yasuo had talked freely about his late employer, and about the two nephews: Toshio whom I had of course met, and his elder brother Koichi about whom I'd heard curiously little. The uncle he described as a nut-case but on the whole a good employer, mainly, I gathered, in the sense that he didn't bother his head overmuch with the fine detail of the housekeeping accounts provided the house was kept spick and span and that his Noh costumes and other gear were treated with due reverence.

Both nephews were familiar visitors to the house but Toshio was in and out of the place more often than his brother, of whom Iida spoke warily, giving Noguchi the impression that he was scared of him. Koichi he described as a tough character, a senior man on the technical side of the computer software company who had little time for anything but shop talk. Iida knew: in his capacity as driver he'd listened in often enough to the conversation when uncle and nephew had been together in the big Nissan car. Koichi always had some office problem or complaint on his mind and was obviously bored stiff when the old man started to talk about his hobby.

Young Toshio was quite different. He must be clever, he was a schoolteacher, wasn't he? Like his girl friend, who came with him sometimes. Nuts about her, Toshio was, anybody could see that. And he could play the piano a treat when he chose to, even though he made some terrible noises when he was sitting there making up stuff of his own, stopping every couple of minutes to scribble on that special music paper. But he was a right dreamer, that one, and the old man must have been barmy to think

96

he could have held down a post in the firm. Good job he never managed to talk the young chap into it, even though he tried often enough. In Yasuo Iida's considered opinion he'd have been fired within a month, family or no family.

Nevertheless, old Suminoe had obviously had a very soft spot for Toshio, and though he often ticked him off it didn't seem to Iida that his heart was in it. Iida was sure that he summoned Toshio to the house so often because he was lonely and enjoyed the young man's company. Toshio had access to the Yamaha piano whenever he liked, and quite often stayed overnight, unlike Koichi, whose wife had never to Iida's knowledge set foot in the place.

I asked Noguchi if Iida had betrayed any anxiety about his own and his wife's future. It seemed not, and this continued to puzzle me rather, but I let it go for the time being. My old friend wasn't supposed to be reporting to me anyway but to his protégé Hara, and I was afraid he might dry up if I started quizzing him.

Needless to say, once Iida was well enough oiled Ninja had invited him to speculate about the identity of the murderer, and about Toshio's motive in trying to commit suicide. No cautious hesitations for Ninja: post mortem or no post mortem, he said he'd referred to the death of Hideki Suminoe as murder, and so, unhesitatingly, had Iida.

Iida the handyman who had, unnoticed, overheard so many of his late employer's conversations, seemed to be prejudiced in Toshio's favour too. He couldn't see him doing violence, it wasn't in his nature. He thought the young man had indeed discovered the body, and been so shattered by the experience, and by his ensuing distress, that he'd blown his top, as Iida put it.

When invited to suggest who might have killed Hideki Suminoe if Toshio hadn't, the man was quite forthright. Oh, Koichi, for sure, he said. Wanted to get his hands on the old chap's money, didn't he?

Now if this were the kind of detective story I like to read myself, I'd never have dropped that bit of information at this stage, would I?

Chapter 15

KNOWING THAT DURING THIS PERIOD OF MY CAREER I WAS stuck with a district prosecutor who liked nothing better than to poke his nose into criminal investigation matters— which unfortunately he was entitled to do—before I was ready to brief him, you're probably wondering what he had to say about all these goings-on.

Needless to say, Prosecutor Akamatsu, or Black Hole as we called him on account of his habit of pursing his lips into an open O shape and concealing his teeth behind them, had wanted to know all about the shooting incident of the second of January as soon as it hit the headlines. He'd sent for Hara, who I'm confident reported the facts as known, and nothing but the facts. If I hadn't happened to be the victim the incident would hardly have merited his personal attention, and unless and until we were in a position to bring charges, Black Hole would simply have to contain his curiosity about it.

The Suminoe murder was in law a different and altogether more serious matter which would certainly have to be reported to him. I'd resolved to call on him as soon as we had the post mortem report and details of anything our forensic specialists had found significant. Actually, remembering the expression on his face when, at his own insistence, he was present when we dug up one of the bodies in the bogus Buddha affair, I'd resisted a passing temptation while at the Suminoe house that memorable Sunday afternoon to give Akamatsu a ring at home and invite him to come and see the corpse in Noh costume for himself.

I could send Hara to report formally to him, but until I'd been officially pronounced fit for normal duty, which I was in no hurry to arrange, he couldn't summon me personally to his office, and he was much too stuffy a man to drop in and see me for a chat. However, one of his assistants had been at the city hall meeting to discuss the matter of the teachers' conference, and word would undoubtedly have got back to him that I was up and about again.

I derived a certain amount of pleasure from our bouts of verbal fencing, but there was no sense in provoking him just for the sake of it; so I rang Akamatsu's private secretary and asked for an appointment to see the great man on the Wednesday, by which time I was confident Hara would have put together a satisfactory briefing document for me to submit to him.

The following day, Tuesday, I didn't feel particularly bright when I woke up, so I reminded myself that I didn't have to put in an appearance at headquarters by any particular time, or indeed at all, for that matter. I began to see distinct advantages in the practice of delegation, and asked Hanae to tell my driver when he arrived to collect me to go and find himself a cup of coffee or something because I wouldn't be ready for an hour or so. Then I took my time over getting myself washed, shaved, and dressed, and read the papers in a leisurely fashion over breakfast, reassuring Hanae that there was nothing particular the matter with me, I simply felt lazy.

We subscribe to two daily newspapers at home: the *Mainichi Shimbun* which is national but whose Osaka edition carries a certain amount of regional news, and the excellent local *Kobe Shimbun*. I get copies of these plus all the other national dailies at my office, of course, but seldom bother to look at them there.

The *Mainichi* had nothing about Suminoe in it, but the local paper informed its readers that "prominent semi-retired local business leader and well-known patron of the Noh theatre Hideki Suminoe (67) died suddenly at his home in Ashiya." There followed a short obituary obviously off their library shelf, accompanied by a head and shoulders photograph allegedly depicting the late Suminoe. Assuming that it did, it must have been taken a good many years earlier, because it showed a proud, confident-looking, fortyish man with all his hair. Wearing a conventional suit, of course.

I was pleased that the paper had left it open to people to assume that Suminoe had died from natural causes. So many relatively young men drop dead in their tracks as a result of stress-induced strokes in Japan these days that reports of sudden death seldom provoke speculation. Nevertheless, I was a little surprised that one or the other of the Iidas hadn't been tempted to gossip to the press, and wondered how long Hara would be able to keep the lid on speculation. The neighbours could hardly have failed to wonder why the police were so interested in the death of an elderly man, however wealthy and well known.

Three cups of coffee put me properly into gear, and by the time I turned up at headquarters I felt reasonably wide awake if not exactly lively. On my desk I found a note from Hara. He'd checked that I had no appointments that morning and wondered if I'd care to accompany him to the office of Susumu Narita, personal legal adviser to our murder victim. The appointment was for eleven-thirty and he, Hara, planned to leave headquarters at eleven-ten.

I looked at my watch. It was just coming up to ten-thirty, so I rang through and told him I'd be glad to go along, and then tried to occupy myself for half an hour with the papers in my in-tray. Most of them needed only acknowledgment or routine approval, so I applied my seal to those and sent

101

them on their way before going down to the lobby and meeting Hara.

The next couple of hours proved to be fascinating. Hara didn't have much to say for himself during the short drive to the law office, in the older part of Kobe where a few blocks of solid, six- and-seven-storey office buildings have so far escaped the attentions of the developers and sit there, squat among their much taller, glossy neighbours. Some of them must be forty years old, which is practically prehistoric for modern urban Japan. I did notice Hara glancing from time to time in the direction of our driver, and it occurred to me that Ninja Noguchi would by then have told him how much old Suminoe's driver Yasuo Iida had gleaned by overhearing conversations between passengers oblivious to his presence.

It was indeed discretion that had made him uncommunicative. No sooner were we out of the car than he told me quickly that the pathologist's report had been received and that there was no doubt whatever that Suminoe had been murdered. He added that, with my permission, he would introduce me not by name and title but simply as a colleague; and I agreed readily. Not expecting to have to walk far, I'd left my stick at headquarters and with luck counsellor Narita wouldn't guess who I was. Then Hara clammed up again as we entered the old-fashioned building which, thank goodness, was equipped with a lift. It was an appropriately vintage specimen which conveyed us in a stately manner to the fourth floor.

"Fourth, eh? Sinister," I remarked. Younger people aren't as superstitious as my generation about the number four, which in Japanese is a homonym for death, but Hara took my point at once and favoured me with a brief smile.

"Times are changing," he confirmed. "Every tall building has a fourth floor, but you won't find many admitting to a thirteenth."

In deference either to Hara's rank or our profession, the lawyer was waiting outside his office door to greet us personally and to usher us directly from the corridor through

102

a door marked "Private" into what was obviously his own room. There the ritual exchange of name-cards took place, except that I accepted one of Narita's when he offered it but of course refrained from returning the compliment. Instead, for no particular reason I glowered at him, and then made my way to a straight chair set against the back wall of the room while Hara muttered something to the effect that his colleague would take notes. This was the first I'd heard of it, and I made no attempt to play up to his suggestion. The only notes I planned to take were of the mental variety.

My disregard for the normal introductory courtesies seemed to have disconcerted Narita, because he darted wary glances at me from time to time while he was settling Hara into the visitor's chair on one side of his big, expensive-looking desk and resuming his own seat on the other, with his back to the windows. I assumed the poker-face for which I understand I'm modestly celebrated, and just sat there, silently looming in the background while Hara chatted brightly about the weather.

Such clichés are of course quite in order until refreshments have been provided, and right on cue the internal door to the outer office was opened and an elegantly groomed young woman entered carrying a tray on which were three cups of coffee, each complete with a little plastic container of cream substitute, a packet of sugar and a cookie in a paper wrapper. I would guess they'd been sent up from a coffee shop in the basement—every sizeable office building has one.

The office lady was well trained, and served Hara first. He gave her a melting smile, which was repaid with interest. The man is practically a sex maniac, I thought, inclining my head gravely and grunting a perfectly civil acknowledgement when my turn came. Finally, as was proper, came her boss; who ignored her, which was unseemly.

I can't think of any particular reason for my having taken such an instant dislike to Susumu Narita, even before he treated his secretary so off-handedly. He was a presentable sort of man, in his early forties by the look of it, and well but not in the least flashily dressed in a good dark suit with a snow-white shirt and a sober necktie. His manner to Hara when eventually they got down to business was helpful and relaxed.

Moreover, his office was a pleasant place to be in. It put me in mind of the sort of attorney's office you see in Hollywood films, with wooden shelving filled with bound legal books occupying most of one wall, and a minimum of visible modern technology. Just an ordinary telephone on Narita's desk, apart from a leather-bound blotter and pen-tray. All it wanted was a framed photograph of a pretty wife and two good-looking youngsters, but, as you know, we Japanese don't go in for that sort of public display. We keep a couple of family snaps in our wallets and show them to bar girls when we get maudlin. But I digress.

In response to Hara's questions, Narita said that Hideki Suminoe had been a client of the firm in which he was a partner for over twenty years, and that he had been personally attending to his affairs for nearly ten. He agreed with a rueful smile that Suminoe had been a very substantial client and that his death was not only a matter for deep personal regret but that the loss of his business would be felt. Though of course the deceased was not exactly a young man at the time of his, er . . .

He went on to confirm that Suminoe had made a secret will under the provisions of the civil code some five years earlier. Suminoe, accompanied by the company secretary of his computer software business, had called by appointment at this very office, bringing with him the hand-written document. This he dated, signed and sealed in the presence of Narita and the other man, who watched him insert it into an otherwise empty envelope, which was securely sealed. The envelope was in turn dated on the outside, and signed by all three men who then impressed their registered personal seals across the flap.

And where was the document kept? On the premises, in

the law office's own strong-room. And who was authorised to open it? The next of kin of the deceased, who would be well advised to do so with witnesses present, especially as the next of kin in this case, Dr. Yoshiko Suminoe, was the only person certain to be a beneficiary.

Even Hara seemed to be unprepared for that, as I was, but Narita went on to remind us that the dead man had never married, and had no children. His own parents had, not surprisingly, died many years earlier. As his only sibling, his sister was therefore entitled under Japanese law to at least a quarter of the estate. Unless, of course, Narita added with a merry little chuckle, she had "ill treated" or "seriously insulted" her brother, or been engaged in "exceptionally reprehensible activities." In that event, according to the civil code, she could be disinherited.

Rather owlishly, Hara agreed that it seemed highly improbable that a well-respected doctor, and moreover one nominated by her brother as his legal personal representative, would turn out to be disqualified. Narita volunteered the information that Dr. Yoshiko—as he breezily called her—had been in touch and was planning to visit him on Thursday to begin the legal formalities. There was little more that Hara could profitably ask at that stage, so he prepared to take his leave and I stood up too.

Having until then given the impression of having all the time in the world for us, Narita all at once seemed anxious to be rid of us. For the last half-minute or so the muffled sound of voices had been emanating from the outer office. No words were distinguishable, but one of the speakers, a man, seemed to be upset about something.

Anyway, Narita bustled Hara out of the door we'd entered by with very perfunctory farewells and assurances of future assistance. As the anonymous note-taking assistant I was expected to trail after them, but I took my time and sauntered over to the big window before doing so. Then I headed for the corridor, slowly enough to see the secretary open and pop her head through the communicating door. She hurriedly withdrew on realising that I was still in the

105

room, but didn't shut the door again quite quickly enough to prevent my catching a glimpse of a man standing just behind her.

It was a very surprising experience for me. The man looked tense and impatient, but more than that, I was sure he was the well-informed bystander who'd been beside me at the special *Okina* Noh performance at the Ikuta Shrine right after Hanae had flared up at me and stormed off on her own. The one who'd explained to me what was going on, and seemed irritated by the way Suminoe had self-importantly drawn attention to himself by his restless manner.

That was something to think about, and there was something else even more interesting. I'd wandered over to the window in order to check out a wild idea that had occurred to me while I was sitting there facing it from the other side of the room; and what I found suggested that perhaps it wasn't all that wild after all. The attorney Susumu Narita's office window commanded a perfect view, between several intervening buildings, of the open space beside the city hall, and of the spot I'd been standing in when I was shot.

I'm long-sighted, and could clearly see the sculpture of the nude girl that I'd been admiring at the time.

Chapter 16

Mindful of Hara's earlier exemplary discretion, during the drive back to headquarters I engaged him in non-controversial chat about the engagement of the Emperor's second son Prince Aya to a professor's daughter, and the National Diet elections to be held in February. Neither subject was of much interest to me, and I found that I could waffle on quite easily while thinking furiously about what I had just experienced.

The location of Narita's office window and the view it commanded were matters of fact. However, I realised that there must be equally good sight-lines to the little park and its nude sculpture from dozens, possibly hundreds of other windows in the vicinity, all well within the range of a good hunting rifle. To argue from the fact that somebody *could* have aimed at me from there to the triumphant conclusion that the culprit had done so would be preposterous. Nevertheless, it was a curious coincidence; another example of the way a Suminoe connection kept suggesting itself.

Then there was the fellow in Narita's outer office, the man whose voice the lawyer had almost certainly overheard and recognised. That surely was the only explanation for his abrupt change of manner and evident eagerness to be rid of us. I couldn't be at all sure about him. Was Narita's fretful visitor in fact my knowledgeable informant at the shrine? After all, I'd caught sight of him for no more than a second or two.

Was I jumping to an unwarranted conclusion on the basis of nothing more than a fleeting impression? The man at the shrine had been dressed in a casual bomber jacket over a sweater, and slacks. I could remember that well enough. Whereas, as you might expect, the man at the law office was wearing a business suit. So far as I could recall, however, they were alike in every other physical respect, much the same build, colouring, facial features, age and so on.

Sitting there in the car, I affably agreed with Hara that young Miss Kiko Kawashima ought to prove to be a welcome new member of the Imperial family, but would have a hard time coping with the iron protocol the officials of the Imperial Household Agency hold so dear. At the same time I was reminding myself that a great deal had happened to me since I'd watched that performance of *Okina* on the second of January.

Trauma was the medical term used to describe what I'd experienced that day. How reliable were the recollections of a traumatised man who in any case had been paying more attention to the performance than to the appearance of a fellow spectator? How eager was I to persuade myself not only that the two men were one and the same, but also and above all that the mystery man was the elder of the nephews, Koichi Suminoe?

By the time we got back to headquarters I was sure of one thing only: that rather than hugging them to myself as I know I'm always inclined to, I was in duty bound to share my thoughts, however absurd, with Hara. So I invited him to come up to my office with me, and told him everything, to his apparent gratification.

For once I was glad of his characteristic earnest pedantry, and appreciated the fact that we both managed to set aside the personal problems that continued to overshadow our official relationship. Hara listened attentively to what I had to say, and took it seriously, analysing my own arguments for and against the possibility of a link between the shooting incident and the Suminoe family in his dispassionate, logical way. He didn't find the notion ridiculously far-fetched.

Then we swapped impressions about Susumu Narita. Hara hadn't taken to him either. He agreed with me that there was something distinctly odd about the way the lawyer had been relaxed and informative one minute and then practically hustled us off the premises the next; and Hara had also heard what sounded like a one-sided altercation in the adjoining office.

There were obvious practical ways in which some at least of the fog could be dispersed. Hara couldn't do any more than I could directly to identify the stranger I'd spoken to at the shrine. On the other hand he was planning to interview Koichi Suminoe himself anyway, and undertook to arrange if possible for me to get a good look at him, or at the very least for me to see a photograph, which might help me to make up my mind.

Hara also promised to get his specialists to go over their earlier work on possible trajectories of the bullet that had hit me. Just to see if there was more than a random chance that it might have come from the direction of Narita's office. Finally, before leaving me he agreed it would in any case be very useful to know something about the background and professional activities of the attorney Susumu Narita.

Conscious of having played fair with Hara and given him no cause to complain that I was meddling, when he'd gone I thought it reasonable to do a certain amount of fossicking about myself. I told myself sternly that if I came up with anything I would of course pass it on immediately, and if I didn't that was my affair. Then I promptly made a nonsense of the alternative possibility by picking up the phone and ringing through to find out if Inspector Jiro Kimura happened to be in the building. I wanted to pick his brains, and besides, I thought an hour or so in his company would provide some welcome light relief after so much of Hara's.

I was in luck. It was late by my standards, nearly one o'clock, but Kimura kept what senior Japanese officials refer to as "French time." He was available, and jumped at my offer to stand him lunch. Well, not quite. He insisted on playing host, and at the Kobe Club, no less. He'd recently become a member of the stately old institution that had once been to all intents and purposes the preserve of expatriate Westerners, and obviously wanted to ensure that I knew.

The clubhouse—to which of course I'd often been taken before—isn't far from prefectural police headquarters, and within fifteen minutes we'd been driven into the spacious grounds and deposited at the main entrance. They weren't all that busy in the dining room, and the head waiter gave us a table in a quiet corner. Kimura beamed expansively as we were handed impressive menus, and recommended the steak with the air of one in the know, adding that he'd been looking forward to celebrating my recovery with me.

In fact, I knew him well enough to be able to detect a touch of hurt pride behind the bonhomie. Since getting out of hospital I'd had virtually no contact with him, and there was no obvious role for him in the Suminoe affair. To put it another way, busy bee Kimura felt left out of things. I told him I'd be happy with a steak, medium rare, and accepted his offer of a gin and tonic, something I enjoy occasionally at lunchtime.

The drinks arrived and Kimura made quite a little speech about how pleased he was to see me back in harness. I was rather touched, and cleared my throat noisily. "Yes. Well, thank you, Kimura-kun. By the way, d'you remember at one of our inner cabinet meetings towards the end of last year you were telling us about, what was it called, garbology? Yes, garbology. Some new American science."

His eyes lit up, as they had when he'd lectured Noguchi, Hara and me about his latest enthusiasm. I was just flattering him when I parroted his own description of what he'd been reading about as a new American science. There was nothing in the least original about the idea of rooting through people's garbage to find out what they get up to, and nothing specifically American about it either, except that according to Kimura some university or other over there had appointed a professor of garbology. Which made it a "science," I suppose, and I reflected that my old father, sometime professor of chemistry at Osaka Imperial University, must be turning in his grave.

"Yes indeed! There's some remarkable work going on in the field," he said, after a long pull at his *jinto*.

"At the rubbish dump, you mean. No doubt, but hardly of much relevance to your present job, I imagine."

Kimura assumed an expression of intimate confidentiality. "You'd be surprised, Chief," he murmured. "You know my man Migishima?"

Of course I knew his man Migishima. Hanae and I had been at the reception following his wedding to Junko, at which Ninja Noguchi, in an ill-fitting, hired morning suit, had improbably officiated as a go-between. In fact Junko, who as a senior detective worked for Hara, outranked her husband, who was assigned to Kimura's foreign residents' section. A beefy, amiable young man who had once during an earthquake tried to save my life. What I mean by that is that it's most unlikely that I would have been killed anyway, but Patrolman Migishima flung himself on top of me with great good will and the best of protective intentions all the same.

"Yes. What about Migishima?" I enquired, and helped myself to a mouthful of really excellent steak.

"Thanks to my encouragement, Migishima's seriously into garbology," Kimura said solemnly, and it was all I could do to keep a straight face.

"Whatever do you mean?"

"Well ... he has a natural flair, I'd say. He's done one or two impressive exercises for me. Of course, it's relatively easier to garbologise in Japan, where householders have always had to separate their rubbish. Ever since I can remember, anyway. In America they're only just getting round to the idea."

111

"Really?" I couldn't remember a time either when I hadn't routinely put out our own household waste to be picked up by the disposal men on different days according to its nature: glass and plastic on Tuesdays, perishable stuff on Fridays and Mondays. In addition to the regular collections, from time to time there are so-called "special garbage" days when people can get rid of bulky unwanted items such as old TV sets and so forth.

"Yes. Well, on his own initiative Migishima got himself up a few times to look like a municipal garbage man and simply picked up a sack or two from outside a house or apartment he knew was occupied by foreigners, before the proper collection men got there. Then he examined the contents and extracted enough data from them to produce a profile of the residents. Without reference to any file information we might have on them, needless to say."

I didn't question Migishima's enterprise or his powers of deduction, but what he had done seemed distasteful to me. "I'm not sure I approve of that, you know," I said, mildly enough since I was Kimura's guest. "Spying on people for the sake of it. It's no better than tapping somebody's phone just out of idle curiosity."

"Not a bit of it. The principle's completely different," Kimura said airily, not in the least abashed. "If Migishima had entered private premises without permission and made a search he would have been completely out of order. But whatever a person chooses to put outside his door for the garbage men is in the public domain."

He was right and I had to agree. "Good point. It still seems a bit unsavoury, but you win, I suppose. Um ... what sort of thing did Migishima find?"

Kimura grinned cheerfully, happy to be one up. "Oh my, you name it, he found it. Old bank statements, receipts, private correspondence, diaries, all manner of financial information. Plus of course empty containers, wrappers, discarded packaging, clothing and so forth that helped him to build up a picture of the person's family situation, domestic habits and life-style." He gazed at me speculatively for a

112

few moments, and then coughed and leant towards me across the table, lowering his voice meaningly. "Want him to go after anybody in particular, Chief?"

"Whatever makes you ask that?"

This time he let out an explosive laugh. "Because this sudden interest in garbology tells me you're cooking something up. Am I right?"

I looked into his bright intelligent eyes for a long moment. "Well, I suppose you could be," I admitted. "But before I go on, do you think I might have another gin and tonic?"

Chapter 17

WHEN I CRAWLED OUT FROM UNDER THE FUTON ON Wednesday morning and went to look out of the south-facing window I saw that there had been a heavy fall of snow overnight. Not unusual at that time of the year, of course: we generally see snow once or twice in January or February in the Kobe area, but it's usually gone again after a day or two, and some winters we get none at all. So it's enough of a rarity to take one by surprise mingled with a touch of childish pleasure at viewing a scene transformed.

My driver was waiting outside the house for me, and he helped me into the car as he had been doing since I got out of hospital, as though I was in the last stages of some mortal illness. Then we were off, and I was rather sorry not to have been able to offer to lend a hand to some children constructing a snow *daruma-san* at the corner of the street. It wasn't a bad one at that, with a couple of yoghurt carton lids for the staring eyes, one of which they'd painted in. The other was presumably due to be added when the project was complete. Time was pressing, however, and on my way to see District Prosecutor Akamatsu I had to drop in at headquarters to pick up copies of Hara's latest progress report on the Suminoe case.

The snow provided a useful subject for the preliminary pleasantries after I'd been shown into Akamatsu's office. The prosecutor made quite a ceremonious fuss about welcoming me for the first time since what he referred to as the "second of January incident," which made it sound very important, like an attempted *coup d'état*.

Black Hole had nothing but praise for the way Hara had kept him briefed while I was out of action, and in my own new, somewhat self-critical mood I reflected that I'd probably made the man's job unnecessarily difficult on many occasions by treating our meetings as exercises in verbal combat: one veteran bureaucrat scoring points off another. We were evenly matched and on the whole I used to enjoy the mental exercise, but one way and another I'd had enough confrontation since the beginning of the year to last me for some time to come. So as soon as we got down to business I handed Akamatsu a copy of Hara's report—which I'd gone through while on the way—and sat patiently while he read it, nodding sagely from time to time.

"Thank you, Superintendent," he said when he'd finished. "An interesting story, set down with admirable clarity and cogency, if I may say so."

"Inspector Hara's reports are exemplary," I agreed, having while looking at the document myself admired Hara's skill in leaving out all the right things while conveying an impression of complete candour.

Laying the report to one side, Akamatsu meshed the fingers of his two hands together and peered at me over the top of his half-glasses, pursing his lips in that weird way of his. "Yes indeed," he said then. "The young man should go far. At least one hopes so, provided that . . ."

I resignedly realised that rumours about Hara's love life must have reached his office, and that he was inviting me to raise the subject, but I certainly didn't feel as cooperative as all that.

"Quite," I said briskly. "Now, Mr. Prosecutor, you'll have appreciated that we now have firm evidence that Hideki Suminoe was indeed murdered."

"So it would seem. But not necessarily by his nephew Toshio."

"Not necessarily."

"Who nevertheless remains the only obvious suspect."

"That is so, I must agree. Though as you have read, he continues to protest his innocence, and we're not confident enough to bring charges against him at this stage. This isn't going to be a routine murder case wrapped up tidily in the usual written confession."

"I see. Not that written confessions are always as reliable as we tend to claim, are they?" I wasn't sure whether that was a dig at the police, who've been known to go to outrageous lengths to extract them, or an admission that public prosecutors are only too ready to accept them without question; so I held my tongue and after a moment Akamatsu went on civilly enough. "Well, Otani-san, what do you propose to do about the young man in the immediate future?"

"Inspector Hara is in charge of the investigation, and I have every confidence in him. In his opinion, which I'm inclined to share, Toshio Suminoe ought to be released from custody on condition that he agrees to remain within the Osaka-Kobe area—living at home with his mother—and to report daily to his local police station while the investigation continues."

Akamatsu nodded. "I see. Clearly his attempted suicide isn't a criminal offence, and in itself doesn't amount to anything like evidence, much less proof that he's a murderer. What does the doctor think?"

"Medical advice is that he's over whatever crisis led to his suicide attempt. Depressed of course, as anybody in his situation would be, but not in the clinical sense. It's thought unlikely he'd do anything silly, and it would probably be good for his state of mind to go back to his teaching job at least for the time being. If you agree to his conditional release we'd keep a discreet eye on him while we follow up other leads."

Akamatsu perked up at that. "You have reason to consider others as possible culprits?"

116

"It would be remiss on our part not to look with particular care at the statements given by the Iidas—the resident servants. Whether or not the nephew's telling the truth, they're in the frame as having had the opportunity. Then we must think about motive, and that brings me to the question of Suminoe's will. You've read Hara's account of our visit to the lawyer?"

"Yes, and I think I can guess what you're going to ask next. You want me to issue a disclosure warrant and authorise an inspection of the secret will."

"Exactly. All we know at the moment is that unless there turn out to be other close relatives whose existence we don't already know about, Suminoe's sister stands to inherit a quarter of the estate. We need to know who else is due to benefit, and where he, she or they were last Sunday."

Black Hole nodded again. He was all sweetness and light that day, and not only agreed at once to my request but in my presence gave instructions to his personal assistant to have the necessary papers drawn up as a matter of urgency. He promised me that the warrant would be served on the attorney Susumu Narita before the end of the afternoon and that as soon as the sealed will was in his possession he would let me know.

"Or should my people inform Inspector Hara? I am anxious to cooperate with you and your staff; and it would, I think, be desirable for you or Hara to be present when I open the envelope. Or indeed both of you if you wish and can spare the time. The contents of the will are, as you've pointed out, bound to be relevant to your enquiries."

"That's very good of you, Mr. Prosecutor. I'll see what Hara thinks."

"Ah, there is one more thing . . ."

"Yes?"

"I gather from this report that the sister of the deceased is to come from Himeji to visit Counsellor Narita tomorrow. I believe that he should be urged to postpone that arrangement. Moreover, I think that if at all possible, any other person likely to be named in the will should be pres-

117

ent at the meeting when it does take place. In fact I may myself wish to attend."

My astonishment must have shown in my face, because Akamatsu leaned forward with the air of one about to whisper a confidence. "You see," he went on, "I am slightly acquainted with Susumu Narita, and I don't trust him an inch."

While on my way to see the prosecutor I'd had no expectations of deriving any pleasure or profit from the visit, but a great deal flowed from the conversation, as you can imagine. When I got back to my own office it was to learn that Hara had gone to the computer software company with an assistant to interview the elder nephew, Koichi. That didn't hold things up significantly, because it was a simple matter to leave a radio message for him with his police driver, and Hara rang me back within half an hour.

After I'd passed on to him the salient points of my discussion with Akamatsu I actually heard him whistle to himself with surprise. Then, brisk and businesslike, he said he'd come straight back to headquarters and sort out the paperwork necessary for the conditional release of Toshio Suminoe as agreed by the district prosecutor. He was as good as his word, and I later learned that the young man was taken home to his desperately worried mother within a few hours. Neither of them was advised that arrangements had been made for the house to be kept under observation by plain-clothes officers and for Suminoe to be followed whenever he went out.

Hara promised to let me know in due course how he'd got on with Koichi Suminoe, but asked if he could deal with various chores first, and of course I agreed. He let me know how to get into touch with him during the next few hours and I tried to get on with some paperwork myself, but not very successfully because I was on tenterhooks waiting for word from the prosecutor's office.

It came just after three in the afternoon, in the form of a laconic call to me from Akamatsu himself. The will had been surrendered, and if one or both of us cared to go over right away . . .

You won't be in the least surprised to learn that Hara and I went together, to find Akamatsu positively snorting with excitement. He told us that the assistant he sent to serve the disclosure warrant on Narita had quite properly gone into the lawyer's outer office and presented his card to the secretary, who took it through the communicating door. Whereupon, after a very brief interval, the assistant prosecutor heard the *other* door being opened, and was just in time to step back into the corridor and intercept Narita, who had obviously been intending to slip away.

"I had warned my man that Narita might seek to evade service of the warrant," Akamatsu said smugly, "and arranged for him to be accompanied by a rather large and burly escort, who was waiting by the elevator. Between them they, ah, persuaded the counsellor to fulfil his legal obligation to hand over the will. Seeing that there was no alternative, he pretended to be eager to cooperate."

I thought it perfectly possible that the man had simply wanted to visit the toilet before receiving his unexpected caller, but the prosecutor clearly saw himself as a ruthless action man, fearless in the face of danger. He seemed to be thoroughly proud of his achievement, and Hara and I made suitable congratulatory noises while we eyed the envelope lying on his desk. It wasn't all that big, but the soft, high quality hand-made paper was bulked out by the contents, and adorned as it was with seals and signatures, it looked like something to be guarded with care.

"Ready, gentlemen?"

Hara and I nodded, and Akamatsu took a pair of scissors from a drawer and neatly snipped off the very edge of one end of the envelope. Then he pulled out a long manuscript folded concertina fashion. You've seen the kind of thing at formal receptions, I'm sure: VIP's read their speeches from them and then hand them over to the host.

The calligraphy was very fine, and for the first minute or

two after Akamatsu opened the paper out the three of us rather got in each other's way, all trying to read it at the same time. Then Black Hole took charge and read it aloud, which was sensible, before summoning a minion and instructing him to make one, and only one, photocopy.

Discounting the formal terminology in which they were couched, the provisions of the secret will were in themselves perfectly straightforward. Hideki Suminoe had confirmed that he had no children whether legitimate or otherwise, and appointed his sister Yoshiko to be his principal executrix, with Narita to assist her, as well as leaving her one third rather than the statutory quarter of his estate.

His branch of the Kanze Noh school was to get his collection of masks and robes, and he made what sounded to me like generous provision for his "valued servants" Yasuo and Emiko Iida. An amount equal, at a rough guess, to at least ten, maybe fifteen years' joint salary and certainly enough to set them up in a little shop or other business if they liked.

All the rest was to go to his "dear nephew" Toshio, who was also to get Dr. Yoshiko's share should she predecease her brother. In the event of Toshio's death "and my own should that occur before I am able to make new testamentary dispositions," his elder brother Koichi, "for whom I have some natural affection," was to be the residuary legatee.

"You realise what this means?" Hara demanded, rather condescendingly I thought, as we left the building. That of course was after we'd thanked Akamatsu and noted his suggestion that sooner or later there ought to be a meeting of all the actual and potential beneficiaries (except the Noh people, whose priorities were hardly such as to lead them to commit murder to get their hands on a quantity of robes and masks a few years earlier than they might otherwise expect to do).

"Of course I do," I said testily. "It means that a great deal hinges on the question, how secret was that secret will? You know, I was expecting Akamatsu to hand that photocopy he had made over to us. Oh well, we know what's in it, that's the main point, I suppose."

"Oh, that reminds me," Hara said. "I have something for you. I picked it up from the waiting room at the software company." He took out a folded leaflet from his inside pocket and handed it over. It was advertising material for the company, boasting about their inhouse expertise, and illustrated by a few photographs of their senior staff. Koichi Suminoe was among them, and after one look at his picture I was no longer in the slightest doubt that he was the man I had spoken to at the shrine the morning I was shot.

Chapter 18

YOU'LL RECALL THAT THE LAWYER NARITA HAD BEEN PLAN-
ning to hand the will over to Dr. Yoshiko Suminoe on the
Thursday following her brother's death. Had there been
nothing untoward about it, the wake, Buddhist rites and cremation would have been completed by then, with a big
public funeral ceremony to follow a week or so later. As
matters stood, however, the body couldn't be released from
the mortuary for a while, and it was now clearly out of the
question for the dead man's intentions to be divulged to
anybody with a financial interest until the mystery of his
murder was cleared up one way or another. In the absence
of a confession that would mean a lot more digging into the
backgrounds and alibis of a number of people, and Black
Hole Akamatsu accepted that this was going to take time.

You must understand that although I'd been sucked into
it and had a strong personal interest in the outcome, the direction of the investigation remained Hara's responsibility,
and during the following few days he and his team undertook all the interviewing and official enquiries. He kept his
promise to keep me in the picture, so I know he called in
whatever outside help he wanted.

The burden of much of the interviewing that he didn't

undertake personally fell on Junko Migishima. She went to Himeji again to see the sister and to enquire discreetly with the help of the local police in that city into her reputation and her movements on the day of the murder. The doctor hadn't seemed to be a very likely suspect from the start, and Junko in effect cleared her in her report, even though she stood to gain a great deal financially by her brother's death.

For as other enquiries progressed, they enabled Hara to build up a reasonably complete picture of the dead man's assets; and it emerged that even after inheritance taxes were deducted the disposable estate was going to amount to a huge sum. I won't attempt to express it in billions of yen which wouldn't mean much to you, so let me just say that it looked as if, when the will was eventually probated, Dr. Yoshiko Suminoe was going to be better off by about fifty times my current annual salary, and young Toshio—if he was cleared of suspicion—was going to be very rich indeed.

The house at Ashiya alone was worth a lot more than even a highly paid business executive such as his elder brother Koichi could hope to earn in a lifetime, his late uncle had built up an impressive portfolio of savings and investments, and there were big life insurance policies, two with Toshio named as beneficiary, and one naming Koichi.

Under the law, if either of the nephews turned out to be the murderer, there could of course be no question of his benefiting. Murder for insurance money is something of a growth industry in Japan these days, and in cases of death in suspicious circumstances we always look very carefully indeed at that aspect of things. The tax authorities would want to take their time over their own investigations, too. When a man admits to being as wealthy as the late Hideki Suminoe, they more or less take it for granted that a lot more money has been directed underground, as we put it, so as to evade taxation. Not for nothing are lawyers and tax accountants notorious for cheating the revenue themselves.

I learned from the daily progress reports that Hara had

left the close interrogation of the two servants, the Iidas, to Ninja Noguchi, and having had a chance briefly to size them up myself I wished I could have been a fly on the wall when he did a thorough job of taking them through their stories, separately, of course.

Like me, Ninja had a nagging doubt about them, but unlike me he voiced it. Like everybody else mentioned in the will, the Iidas were supposed to be ignorant of its provisions. That was the whole point about a secret will. Yet they still seemed completely unworried about their long-term future. True, they were secure for the next few months at least, for it was soon established that the lady doctor from Himeji had been in touch and asked them to stay on and take care of the house until further notice and had agreed to pay their salaries and expenses, which seemed fair enough in the circumstances.

It wasn't really enough to make them carefree, though, and I toyed with the idea that Iida might conceivably have been paid handsomely to kill his employer, with his wife to cover for him. Or *vice versa*, of course. If there was anything in it, that would open up the field with a vengeance, so I decided not to try it on Hara until he'd found out as much as he could about the obvious suspects.

He interviewed both nephews on a number of occasions during those few days, without inviting me to be present. Toshio felt confident enough to return to his teaching job, and otherwise appeared to be staying quietly at home. He duly reported to his local police station every day, and remained adamant that he was innocent.

As for his elder brother Koichi, Hara indicated to me that he went to great pains to avoid giving him the impression that he was suspect in any way. Hara found him tough-minded but, as he put it, cooperative; admitting that he and his uncle had frequently argued, but insisting that their relationship had been basically friendly. Koichi also volunteered the information that on the Sunday of the murder he had been at home in the company of his wife and two children all day; and hardly surprisingly his wife independently confirmed that. It meant virtually nothing.

What was of some interest to me was to learn from Hara that Koichi made no bones about his disapproval of his younger brother: indeed his contempt for him. In a way this helped young Toshio's case, such as it was. Invited to suggest who might have had a motive to kill Uncle Hideki, Koichi said the old man had offended any number of people over the years, including Toshio whom he was forever bullying, but insisted that although things looked black for Toshio because he had obviously had the opportunity, he was far too much of a milksop to commit murder. Koichi said that on the other hand his brother's suicide attempt hadn't surprised him at all. It wasn't the first time Toshio had made what Koichi implied was an insincere gesture.

From where I was sitting it began to look as if Hara was facing stalemate. Only about sixteen or seventeen hundred murders in all Japan come to the attention of the police in an average year, and all but a few dozen are cleared by arrests, almost always made on the basis of a confession. Unsolved murders are therefore practically unheard of, and the victims in the few cases that defeat us are, as you might expect, generally derelicts of one sort or another about whom nobody much cares in life or death.

The district prosecutor certainly wasn't going to shrug his shoulders philosophically over an admission of failure to find the murderer of a man such as Suminoe, however. Nor would he agree to the arrest on the basis of purely circumstantial evidence of a well-connected man who only opened his mouth in order to insist that he was innocent. By the beginning of the following week I had more or less decided that the situation was serious and unpromising enough for me to take over the direction of the case personally. This wasn't because I was so arrogant as to suppose that I could do any better than Hara, but simply because he had his career ahead of him while mine was practically over. I had nothing except a certain amount of self-esteem to lose if I failed.

I passed a quiet weekend at home, enjoying relative peace on the domestic front. Things were by no means back to what I nostalgically thought of as pre-row contentment. Hanae and I were too self-consciously polite to each other for that. Nevertheless we seemed to be getting along a lot better following the excitements of the previous weekend, and once or twice Hanae mentioned that she had been talking to Michiko on the phone most days and that her sister was, as she put it, thinking things through. Judging by the official pressure Hara was under, it struck me as unlikely that he was in a position to spare much time to join her in that exercise, but I knew it wouldn't help the situation for me to say so.

In retrospect I'm very glad I put off my decision to intervene in the investigation until after the weekend, because when I turned up at headquarters rather late on Monday morning, it was to learn that Kimura wanted to see me urgently. I rang through to him at once and less than five minutes later he burst excitedly into my office clutching a large brown envelope and virtually towing a bashfully reluctant Migishima in his wake.

"Breakthrough, Chief!" he chirruped, before remembering that he was accompanied by a humble patrolman, coughing and assuming a slightly more formal manner. "That is, good morning, sir. I'm pleased to report that Migishima here has struck oil, as it were. So I took the liberty of bringing him up here with me."

The moment I'd heard Kimura was asking to see me I'd assumed it was in connection with the garbological researches I'd instigated over lunch at the Kobe Club, so I was as eager to listen as he was to talk. Kimura flopped uninvited into the single visitor's chair facing my desk, while Migishima stood rigidly to attention not far from the door. He was always painfully shy in my presence even though we knew each other pretty well. I can only assume that the reason why such a lively minded person as his wife Junko was happy with him was that his private persona was completely different from the one I encountered. I thought

126

about urging him to relax and sit down but decided he was probably best left where he was.

"Good morning, Inspector. And to you, Migishima. Well, don't keep me in suspense. What have you got for me?"

Kimura deposited the envelope on my desk and I looked at it warily. "It's all right," he said, seeing my expression. "I mean, nothing smells bad or anything like that. Besides, Migishima put the individual items in separate bags."

Still dubious, I removed the clip which was all that kept the envelope closed, turned the flap back and upended it so that the contents slithered out. There were in all seven plastic bags, each neatly labelled.

"Three from the garbage of Koichi Suminoe's place, four from Susumu Narita's house."

I looked directly across at Migishima and actually managed to catch his eye. He was beaming and nodding in support of his inspector. "Well done," I said, and then turned my attention to his haul, sorting them into two groups. In hatching my little plot with Kimura I'd stressed that neither of the two men I was curious about was likely to be so obliging as to leave anything really incriminating lying about at home. After all, they both worked in offices likely to be equipped with shredders.

On the other hand, they both had wives who might all innocently in the course of tidying their houses throw out items of some interest. Prosecutor Akamatsu had been good enough to tell me in personal confidence that Narita was married and where he lived, and of course we already knew Suminoe's address. After a brief survey of what had come from their discarded rubbish bins I felt quite embarrassed to recall that I'd spoken lightly of garbology.

Migishima had retrieved from Narita's household refuse two small-circulation right-wing magazines of recent date, and an ill-printed leaflet calling on all "patriots" to "cleanse the city of Kobe of the communist filth who corrupt the minds of our children." The date, time and place of what was referred to as a "rally for effective action" at the time of the teachers' union conference were given. I was quite

127

sure that copies were already in the hands of our riot police commanders, but certainly wouldn't have expected a busy attorney to have one at home.

The fourth item was a mere slip of paper which meant nothing to me until I turned it over in its transparent bag and saw that it was a printed band of the type used in banks to secure bundles of notes. This particular one, which bore the issuing bank's date and certification stamp, had, no more than a few days ago, been wrapped round a stack of no less than a hundred ten-thousand-yen bills. Worth in all about four thousand of your English pounds or seven thousand American dollars, I think. Not exactly a fortune, but hardly to be thought of as housekeeping money, either.

That alone was a thought-provoking haul and one calling for congratulations, but Migishima had surpassed himself at the elder Suminoe nephew's residence. One of the three items from there was also a magazine, this time aimed at outdoor sportsmen, by which it meant hunters. The second was an empty, flattened cardboard box which had once contained rifle bullets, and the third was best of all.

It was a smoothed-out, previously crumpled sheet off a telephone note pad. Suminoe's wife must be a frugal soul, who disposed of each sheet only when there was no room on it for any more notes and messages. Most of the scribbles with which the sheet was covered looked humdrum enough, but there were also names and phone numbers that might well turn out to be relevant to our enquiries.

One in particular most certainly was. The note was in a childish hand, addressed to "Dad," and read as follows: "Narita-sensei rang. He wants to talk to you. Important."

Chapter 19

THE ESTABLISHING OF A LINK BETWEEN KOICHI SUMINOE AND the lawyer Narita constituted an encouraging breakthrough. The revelation that Narita was at least interested in the activities of the extreme political right and had on a recent occasion had some reason to be in possession of a large sum of money in cash was interesting and suggestive, but didn't lead my thoughts immediately in any particular direction.

The empty carton which had originally contained bullets and the magazines that clearly pointed to Koichi Suminoe as a marksman were a find indeed, and all in all I felt rather pleased with myself for having instigated Migishima's researches. The achievement was, however, undoubtedly his, and after asking him a few detailed questions about his methods I congratulated him warmly before, to his manifest relief, letting him escape from the room.

When I was alone with Kimura I thanked him for his effective and discreet handling of my little private project, and decided to share a few immediate thoughts with him.

"Two points about Migishima first, Kimura-kun. If—and this is entirely up to you, of course—if you feel inclined to suggest that he deserves a formal commendation, or even that the time has come for him to be promoted, I'll be delighted to approve a submission from you."

Kimura's a generous-minded soul and he looked so pleased that I might almost have been proposing an official pat on the back for himself. "Terrific, Chief. I'll get on to it right away. Just one thing, though, um, I mean, I wouldn't have to lose Migishima, would I? If he moves up a notch?"

"I shouldn't think so. But that does bring me to the problem I seem to have created."

Kimura didn't say anything, but his eyebrows shot up enquiringly.

"An organisational problem," I went on. "This is Hara's case, and I don't want to interfere. But obviously I've already done so, and involved you into the bargain. This material Migishima has come up with is first class and makes the whole investigation look much more promising. It must obviously be given to Hara right away. Well, what I'm wondering is this. Inasmuch as Junko Migishima is already working closely with Hara on the Suminoe case, might it be a good idea to let it be thought that her husband and she cooked up the garbology project between them?"

Kimura looked genuinely puzzled. I was surprised, having every reason to know he's normally quick on the uptake. "It would keep me in the clear so far as Hara's concerned, you see. The thing is, I think that thanks to these discoveries we're moving into a phase where we're all going to have to lend a hand openly in order to flush out our murderer, but I'd like the suggestion to come from Hara."

This time Kimura grinned, and after a moment I smiled too. "All right," he said then, cheerfully. "If that's the way you want to play it. It might take a while for me to get the idea over to Migishima, but Junko won't need telling twice."

I put the collection of interesting items from the Narita and Suminoe household refuse in their plastic bags back into the big brown envelope and pushed it over to him. "I don't want to know *how* you organise things or what story you cook up, but make sure Hara gets the specialists to have a look at the bullet carton right away. Meantime I shall look through my in-tray while waiting patiently to be invited to a full briefing conference and tactical planning meeting to be chaired by the head of criminal investigation section in the very near future. I might have one or two suggestions to offer if asked for my views."

An hour or so later Hara rang to tell me that there had been interesting developments, and that he'd called a round-table conference for that same afternoon. He hoped I could find time to be present. He didn't propose that we should meet in my room, and I could see why he wouldn't. He gave me the details, and in due course I made my way to a conference room on the second floor that I must have been in more than once over the years. I hadn't however the slightest recollection of ever seeing the room before, and reflected that considerable chunks of the building in which I'd worked for many years were virtually unknown territory to me.

When I showed up at the appointed place a minute or two before the time I'd been given, Hara rose courteously to greet me, apologised for disrupting what he unblushingly referred to as my busy schedule—as if I'd have missed this meeting for the world—and wondered aloud if I would be good enough to occupy the vacant chair immediately to his right.

There were five others present, all standing up out of deference to me. Even Ninja Noguchi, who was to Hara's right, next to Kimura who was looking slightly sardonic. Junko Migishima and her large husband were further down the table, and I noticed that she coloured slightly when her eyes met mine. There were a couple of unoccupied places between the Migishimas and a scruffy-looking man I didn't immediately recognise, introduced by Hara as Detective Noda. When I heard the name I recalled that he was the officer working under cover to keep an eye on a group of

131

suspected radical activists, which accounted for his appearance.

It was obvious to me that Hara must have started his meeting some time before I'd been invited to join in, and I suppose I ought to have been offended. In fact the unfamiliar surroundings and the formality of the set-up just made me feel detached; almost as if I was dreaming it all.

Looking back, I have to say that Hara stage-managed the whole thing very effectively. I shall probably never know what passed between him and Kimura, or for that matter between Kimura and the Migishimas, but the presence of Detective Noda who was in a sense an outsider ruled out any reference to garbology as such, or how it came to constitute a method of enquiry in this case.

In the course of a beautifully organised, ten-minute summary of the background to the Suminoe murder, with descriptions of the people seemingly concerned and an account of the progress of the investigation, Hara referred to Migishima's haul simply as "significant material evidence obtained as a result of meticulous and imaginative investigative work." I stared up at the ceiling during that bit, preferring not to intercept any exchanges of meaningful glances.

Summing up, Hara stressed the significance of the secret will and the strong possibility that the motive of the murderer was likely to have been financial. He pointed out that so far as opportunity was concerned, the younger nephew Toshio Suminoe was the clear front-runner but that Yasuo Iida and his wife Emiko were also obvious suspects. So was the elder nephew Koichi Suminoe who as a frequent visitor to the house was familiar with the layout and might well have possessed himself of a doorkey. He lived comparatively nearby and his alibi, depending wholly on his wife's word, was not necessarily to be relied on. Finally, it must be borne in mind that in any situation involving members of a family and their dependents and associates and with a great deal of money at stake the possibility of conspiracy must be carefully considered. One or both of the resident servants might have killed their employer at the behest of a family member or even the lawyer Susumu Narita, who was, to say the least, in an equivocal position. At that point Hara turned to me and invited me to comment.

"Thank you, chairman," I began, doing my best to maintain the formal tone. "I have nothing to add to your summary and analysis of the murder of Hideki Suminoe. I should, however, like to deal with what initially seemed to be a completely unrelated issue, namely the bullet wound I sustained on the second of January. I now believe that I was not in fact the intended victim, but that Toshio Suminoe was. He was in the vicinity at the time, and indeed gave a statement as a witness. Now it happens that his uncle Hideki had a couple of hours earlier participated in an open-air Noh performance or ceremony at the Ikuta Shrine. I was there and saw it."

There was a bottle of mineral water and a glass in front of me, and I paused to pour myself a drink before going on. "The murdered man was, we have learned, in the habit of requiring or persuading his nephew Toshio to assist him and watch him rehearse his Noh chanting and dancing. It seems possible that Toshio was in central Kobe not far from the Ikuta Shrine on that day because he had accompanied his uncle and possibly helped him with his costume. I didn't notice him among the spectators at the performances, but he might of course have been there. I know his elder brother Koichi was, because I quite fortuitously fell into conversation with him."

This was no news to the senior people at the table, of course, but both Noda and Migishima shifted in their seats when I came out with it. "My wound was, I am advised, inflicted by a bullet from a hunting rifle, and having visited the law office of Susumu Narita in the company of Inspector Hara here I can confirm that it is *possible*—I put it no more strongly—that it was fired from Narita's window—" Hara interrupted me with a cough.

"The Superintendent is, I know, aware that the new evidence I mentioned suggested strongly that one of Koichi

133

Suminoe's hobbies is hunting. Within the last hour a check through the records has confirmed that he possesses a duly licensed high-powered rifle. We now also have reason to believe that Suminoe and Narita are associated in some confidential way." He smiled at me rather sadly. "It may save time if I mention this myself."

"Oh. I see. Very well, then." There wasn't much more to be said about that, so I just pressed on. "It isn't fanciful to speculate that either Koichi Suminoe or Narita himself might have fired that shot from the office window, and no doubt arrangements will be made for the hypothesis to be tested by experts. Now I can think of no reason why either of them should have wanted to shoot me; but on the other hand I can't explain how, if Toshio was the intended victim, he was persuaded to turn up at a particular time and conveniently place himself in the line of fire. Nor, assuming that he did, can I understand why the marksman missed him and winged me instead. All I can suggest is that, given what we know about the contents of the will, his brother Koichi certainly stood to gain a great deal of money by killing Toshio."

Kimura and Hara both started to talk at once after that, and to my satisfaction the whole tone of the meeting altered in the sense of becoming much more relaxed. A general discussion ensued, during which Junko Migishima, never one to be tongue-tied in the presence of senior officers, pointed out that killing Toshio first might have put the whole plan in jeopardy, since Hideki could have altered the provisions of his will unless he too were disposed of very shortly afterwards. Kimura countered that by arguing that killing Toshio first would tend to divert suspicion, and that if Koichi was ruthless enough to do it he certainly wouldn't have any scruples about going straight on to murder his uncle, perhaps making it look as though the old man's grief led to a heart attack. Suffocation if set about in the right way could be disguised easily enough, he thought.

Ninja Noguchi made only one contribution, growling that if Kimura and I were both right we ought to keep an eye

134

on Toshio in case his brother had another go at him. While there was still time, as he put it.

I'd been wondering why Detective Noda had been summoned to the meeting, and my curiosity was satisfied when Hara brought us all to order and asked him what he thought about it all. Noda seemed to be quite ready to talk, and I soon learned why. He began by saying that he had been brought into the enquiry by Inspector Hara on the day following the murder. Toshio Suminoe had been taken into custody and, noting that he was a school teacher, Hara had wanted to know if he had any record of political activism. Quite why he should have thought for a moment at that early stage that there might be a political dimension to the affair I can't imagine. I was nevertheless much impressed by this evidence of Hara's determination to find out without delay all he could about the number one suspect.

Noda's enquiries yielded the information that Suminoe was a member of the All-Japan Teachers' Union and held minor office as secretary of his school's branch, but that he was not known to hold or voice strong political opinions. Indeed, inasmuch as he had a reputation at all it was as a conscientious, idealistic soul who was temperamentally averse to extremism of any kind.

Noda reminded us that the teachers were to hold their annual conference in Kobe very shortly and that the usual noisy opposition was only to be expected from the rightists, who were thought to be planning some sort of dramatic gesture. A close eye was being kept on them and on the radical extremists on the left whom it was his job to observe. Noda had heard of Susuma Narita as a lawyer willing to represent clients charged with public order offences, but was not aware that Narita himself was of any particular interest to the Public Security Investigation Agency.

By the time Hara brought the discussion to a close, it was obvious that several avenues remained to be explored. It was equally clear that Koichi Suminoe and Susumu Narita were now strongly suspected of something even if we weren't quite sure what it was, and that every effort

135

should be made to close an investigative net round the pair of them. There was general agreement that while this was going on, they should so far as was humanly possible be kept in ignorance of our activities, and even encouraged to think that our suspicions were mainly directed at others.

I was probably the most vocal in urging that view; and I have never ceased to reproach myself for doing so.

Chapter 20

"MEANTIME, THE POLICE CONTINUED WITH THEIR METICU-lous investigations." I remember reading that years ago in a translation of an English detective story, and thinking at the time that it's a useful shorthand phrase for a writer. It's enough to get the reader's imagination working, but spares him or her (you notice how careful I am these days not to be sexist) a lot of boring irrelevancies. I could go into great detail about the way Hara and the others during the next two or three days followed up all the leads mentioned or discussed at his round-table conference, but since I didn't personally do any of the work, most of the information I could supply would of necessity be second or third hand. While happy for others to make the often tedious, some-times frustrating and only occasionally fruitful enquiries en-tailed, however, I was of course deeply interested in the results.

Some important facts were established beyond serious question. Our ballistics specialists confirmed that the bullet Dr. Sugawara extracted from my back had been of the make and type contained in the empty box retrieved by Migishima from Koichi Suminoe's garbage, and the stocks of licensed ammunition dealers in the area were being checked to identify which one had sold that particular batch. We still wanted to allow Suminoe a good deal of rope, however, so the decision to impound his rifle and go for a definite match was deferred.

In collaboration with the investigators attached to the local tax office, Narita's financial affairs were looked into, and it became clear that substantial sums in cash were not infrequently drawn from a bank account maintained not in his own name but that of his wife. Other confidential enquiries revealed that Toshio Suminoe's modest finances were in scrupulous order, and that his aunt Yoshiko in Himeji seemed always to pay the taxes due on her own substantial professional earnings promptly and down to the last yen.

By contrast, a year or so earlier Koichi Suminoe had taken out a huge loan against the security of his house. Even so, he seemed to be perennially short of money, and Ninja Noguchi learned through one of his disreputable contacts that he was a frequent heavy gambler at illicit mahjongg clubs.

In short, our suspicions were being confirmed and the net was being drawn ever closer, but not quite fast enough, as you'll hear. Because I can't put this off any longer. I have to tell you now about that terrible opening day of the teachers' conference, and the moment when I would have given anything to be able to put the clock back and re-run the crucial few minutes differently.

All nature seemed to be weeping bitterly from the start. It was raining heavily in Rokko when I was picked up from my house in the morning, and by the time I arrived in central Kobe it was simply bucketing down. It didn't make any difference to the riot police on duty outside the municipal hall in which the conference was due to begin at ten. Their protective blue coveralls, gauntlets and helmets with the heavy gauge plastic visor are proof against fire, acid and brickbats of various kinds, so mere rain was scarcely even a minor irritant.

For the dozens of ordinary uniformed police on duty in the area the foul weather was much more of a nuisance, but even they had their black oilskins on, and peaked caps to divert the rain from their faces. It was the plain-clothes officers who really suffered, because they obviously couldn't encumber themselves with umbrellas, and ordinary raincoats simply couldn't cope with hour after hour of the downpour. I'm tempted to include myself among the hard-done-by, but as a matter of fact I spent a lot of the time keeping dry and warm in the riot police chief's command van. Of my own closest colleagues I knew only that Ninja Noguchi would be somewhere around, and Kimura had said he planned to be there some of the time with Migishima, mainly to see if any foreigners tried to get involved. Japanese law forbids aliens to take part in open-air political demonstrations.

Needless to say, the demonstrators on both sides got thoroughly sodden, but the weather didn't deter them. It did, however, keep away most of the casual bystanders who normally turn up on these occasions, which was all to the good, and during the greater part of the morning things went much as we'd expected them to. The whole city block in which the hall was located had been closed to normal road traffic, and the rightists weren't allowed to park their ugly trucks festooned with Rising Sun flags and painted slogans anywhere. So they cruised endlessly, and quite legally of course, round and round the perimeter, their loudspeakers blaring.

Delegates to the conference obviously had to have access to the building, and could get to it through a check-point manned by police and teachers' union marshals at the east end of the block. Anti-union demonstrators on foot were kept well away from the hall itself, being required to remain behind barriers set up at the western end of the street in which it stood, about a hundred metres away from the main entrance. One of the armoured riot police buses was parked there, just inside the barriers, with the command van next to it. So whenever I chose to look out of its window, or indeed at one of the video monitoring screens inside, I had a good view of the core group of about a hundred drenched rightists who were marching up and down on their side shouting their heads off.

It was the sort of crew I'd seen often enough before. All were men, the majority of them in their twenties and thirties, much too young to have any memories likely to be stirred by the wartime marches and patriotic songs booming out from the vehicles being driven round by their more privileged associates. These younger thugs in their heavy boots, jeans and leather bomber jackets looked on the whole stupid rather than wicked; with vacuous expressions even while they were raggedly echoing the slogans bellowed by their leader through a bullhorn fitted with an amplifier. To tell you the truth, they put me in mind rather of your English soccer hooligans that we see on television. I doubt if they had a political idea as such among the lot of them. They were just the chorus, though; there to make up the numbers. Dotted among them were a dozen or so older, hard-eyed men who knew very well what they were about, and were the ones that needed watching with special care. Beyond the demonstrators a fair-sized crowd of nondescript male bystanders had assembled in spite of the weather, and I remember thinking that some of them might well be sympathisers: a sort of reserve to be drawn on if necessary.

At that stage, during the opening ceremony and subsequent speeches, virtually all the teachers' union delegates were inside the hall. So as not to leave the field completely clear for the opposition, however, a group of about twenty unionists had positioned themselves outside the entrance to the hall—but sensibly under the canopy out of the rain—and were jeering back at the demonstrators. I imagine they'd been selected for their size, since they were mostly big men, and with their red headbands they looked as though they could take pretty good care of themselves; not that we had the slightest intention of letting them try.

It was a stalemate of a kind, and after an hour or so I

was beginning to wonder if there was the slightest point in my being there, when the situation deteriorated very suddenly. The union delegates had been advised not to leave the hall before the adjournment at the end of the afternoon, when arrangements had been made for them to be taken in buses under police escort to a safe dispersal point. The organisers had, we'd been assured, provided refreshment and other facilities for all participants inside the building so that they could remain safe and comfortable on the premises during breaks.

What exactly went wrong with the plan I don't know. Maybe the incessant din kicked up by the rightists which must have been all too audible inside the hall eventually got on people's nerves, or maybe a few hotheads among the teachers themselves decided, against the advice of their union leaders, to give the demonstrators a taste of their own medicine. All I can testify as a privileged observer is that at shortly before noon several dozen delegates wearing headbands and including a good many women seemed to boil out of the entrance to the hall, pushing past their own tough doorkeepers. Within moments they had formed up and started a frenzied and thoroughly ill-judged snake dance in the street outside. It seemed to have been improvised on the spur of the moment, because they carried no placards, just zig-zagged from side to side in a ragged column, each holding on to the waist of the one in front and yelling taunts and insults at the opposition. The rightists in response surged up against the police barriers that had so far contained them, and those at the front tried to overturn them.

It was a tricky situation, but one that could probably have been brought under control fairly quickly by the riot police reinforcements who almost immediately poured into the area on foot from their parked buses nearby. Those men know their job, and with the aid of their heavy wooden staves and support if needed from the mobile water cannon trundling up in their wake ought to have been able to separate the rival groups in short order. That they weren't able

141

to was because a few of the snake-dancing unionists swayed just close enough to the barriers to enable a tall young rightist to reach out, first grab hold of the sleeve of one of the women teachers and then drag her bodily over to the other side of the barriers where the poor creature was at least temporarily surrounded by mauling, punching, crudely jeering men.

Within seconds a couple of uniformed officers and a lone riot policeman who happened to be in the vicinity were fighting their way into the *mêlée* to rescue the teacher. There was nothing I could personally do to help, except by getting out of the way of the riot police commander who needed easy access to all his communication equipment. So I removed myself immediately from his control van.

It was as I emerged through the open door and clambered down the fold-out stairs into the rain that I saw with what I can only describe as sick disbelief that Toshio Suminoe was one of the snake dancers, and that he was tearing himself free from the companions who were trying to restrain him. Then he shot past me, sprinting towards the struggling, still-captive woman while emitting a kind of animal howl that I could hear quite clearly in spite of the racket going on all around. Then I saw Migishima of all people, in plain clothes and running from the opposite direction to intercept Suminoe, bellowing, "No, *No!*"

When I see that scene again in my mind's eye as I do over and over again, it's as though it were being played in slow motion. In fact I suppose it took no more than a couple of seconds for Migishima to reach and bodily seize the slightly built man, at the precise moment that I heard the unmistakable report of a gun.

In all the continuing confusion not many could have noticed exactly what happened then, but for me both the noise and the pitched battle that developed between the police and both sets of demonstrators faded completely away, and I had eyes only for the two men in the roadway, staggering in what looked like an insane sequence of dance steps before they fell together to the glistening roadway. As I has-

142

tened towards them I saw Suminoe move and apparently try to extricate himself from Migishima's grip. But Migishima lay still, blood pouring from a hideous wound in his head and being washed immediately away by the relentless rain.

Others were there before me. Expert hands were laid on Migishima, and through my fog of shock and misery I heard the siren wail of the approaching ambulance. I stood there uselessly as they lifted him on a stretcher and took him away. Toshio Suminoe was being half restrained, half supported by a couple of uniformed officers, and our eyes met. He looked dazed but otherwise seemed unhurt. Then he looked over my shoulder and I saw an expression of pure horror freeze his features.

Turning, I recognised the burly figure of Ninja Noguchi a few yards away, and as he approached through the still-milling mass of demonstrators and riot police I saw that his face was set like stone and that he had Toshio's brother Koichi by one arm twisted up behind his back in an unbreakable lock. Noguchi is still an immensely powerful man in spite of his age, and for all that the elder Suminoe brother was at least twenty-five years younger and was himself a well-built man, he was writhing helplessly and in obvious pain. A little behind them another man was being propelled roughly by two uniformed officers towards the police command van.

Chapter 21

An hour or so later I knew more or less what had happened and why, but I think the minds of all of us who sat there in a small private waiting room they'd provided for us at the hospital were focused on the unseen battle being waged nearby for the life of Ken'ichi Migishima.

Junko, his wife, usually so full of life, sat unmoving, bundled in a voluminous raincoat she refused to take off though the room was warm and stuffy. Her little urchin face, on which I'd so often seen an expression of cheeky impishness, looked pinched and deathly pale. Sitting on her right, a uniformed policewoman had been murmuring well-intentioned words of comfort and reassurance, but after a while I noticed Junko shake her head almost imperceptibly and I raised a finger to my own lips to signal the girl to desist.

Ninja Noguchi was sitting on the other side of Junko, saying nothing. He was obviously still wet through, and frankly the odour given off as his shabby clothing began to dry was far from delightful. The predominant hospital smell competed with it reasonably effectively, however, and in any case he simply rose above such mundane considerations by the massive strength of his presence. Even I was struck by the fact that he seemed to generate great waves of tenderness.

He had Junko's left hand enfolded in his great calloused paw, but hadn't uttered a word since we entered the room. It was Ninja's privilege to be Junko's principal supporter at this time, for he had been go-between at her wedding and thereby assumed a lifetime duty of care and concern for her and her husband. Hara as Junko's boss would have liked to be there and had sent a message of sympathy, but he had his hands full dealing with the Suminoe brothers and I'd told him I'd take charge at the hospital end.

Kimura sat beside me, trying as always to be positive. He'd been the last to enter the room, having been talking to the medical superintendent.

"They called in Professor Adachi from the university and he rushed here within minutes," he murmured. "They were lucky to get hold of him. I'm told he's regarded as the top brain surgeon in the region."

"Really? That's good," I said dully, hardly registering what he was saying.

"And a first-rate consultant anaesthetist was on the premises anyway. Oh, this will interest you, your Dr. Sugawara is assisting."

That did catch my attention. Quite apart from the tension and anxiety I felt over Migishima, it was a strangely unnerving experience to be back in the hospital where I'd been cared for myself not so many weeks earlier, and in superficially similar circumstances at that. It was curiously comforting just then to know that the prickly but totally unpompous woman who had stretched out on the floor so that I could see her was helping Junko's husband.

"Well, she did a fine job for me," I said at the very moment the door was opened and a young woman in ordinary office worker's clothes came in. She went straight over to Junko, who looked up at her, eyes wide with apprehension.

"Mrs. Migishima, would you mind coming with me for a moment, please? Professor Adachi would like a word with you on your own."

145

Junko nodded and swallowed, then disengaged her hand from Ninja's, stood up and followed the secretary or whoever she was out of the room. A moment later Ninja lumbered to his feet too. "I'll wait for her outside," he growled. I nodded and watched him blunder out of the room. Then I sighed and turned to Kimura.

"It can only be bad news, Kimura-kun."

"I reckon so. Please God don't let him live as a helpless vegetable."

So far as I know Kimura was and is totally irreligious and I was surprised to hear him utter what sounded to me like a Christian prayer. He fell silent but the muscles of his mouth worked as he sat there. I shared the feelings he'd expressed, remembering that Migishima was not only a big fellow but was also appealingly clumsy, or at least had been as a young recruit when I first encountered him. I don't presume to guess what influence Junko had on him during their few years of marriage: I am certain, though, that it must have been wholly good.

Working for Kimura must have undoubtedly done a lot to sophisticate Migishima. He had, I knew, added a useful command of English to his understanding of German, and the spectacular results of his garbological activities suggested that he had a nimble mind. Then I saw him again in my mind's eye as he had been so recently in my office, standing there rigidly at attention and beetroot-red in the face, and was glad some at least of his naivety and awkwardness had stayed with him. It somehow went with his eager, enthusiastic spirit. There must have been appalling brain damage from that wound, though, and it was heartbreaking to think that the gauche, fiercely loyal young man might be destined to . . . it didn't bear thinking about.

"It's silly to guess like this, when we shall find out before long," I burst out abruptly and over-loudly, talking for the sake of talking, I suppose in an attempt to shut out the thoughts Kimura's words had inspired in my own mind. My banal remark broke a longish silence and must have made the young policewoman jump, because she sat up abruptly

146

and when I caught her eye she looked acutely embarrassed. So I spoke directly to her, moderating my voice. "By the way, I'm sure Migishima-san's glad you're here, even if she didn't feel like talking. I expect—"

The door was opened again, and this time Dr. Sugawara came in, still wearing her green theatre gown and cap, her surgical mask dangling below her chin. The expression in her face and her limp posture when she sank into the chair Junko had been occupying made words hardly necessary, so I wasn't impatient when after glancing at each of us in turn she remained silent for several seconds before turning her face to me and speaking.

"They told me you were here, Otani-san."

"Yes. Hello, Doctor."

"He's gone, I'm afraid. There was never—I mean, we did our best, you know—"

"Of course you did. We're all deeply grateful."

"But it was hopeless from the start, really."

"Yes." Kimura was sitting there looking completely stricken, and I realised that my own grief must be apparent in my face.

"You'd think that somebody in my job would get inured to this kind of thing, but it's always upsetting to lose a patient." Dr. Sugawara blinked a couple of times and then looked at me more attentively. "Anyway, you seem to have mended well enough if you're back at work full-time and in weather like this. That's something, isn't it?"

"Thanks to you, Doctor. Yes, I suppose it is. All the same, I'd gladly have traded my life for that young man's."

"The way medicine's going, people might be given that option not so many years from now. I hope I'm never put in the position of having to offer it to anybody. You must excuse me now, I have other patients to attend to." Dr. Sugawara sighed as she straightened up and wearily got back to her feet.

"Of course. It was good of you to come and tell me. Please pass on my respects to Professor Adachi and all the theatre staff," I said as we all three stood as well out of respect, the policewoman also saluting Dr. Sugawara smartly. She acknowledged the salute and Kimura's and my bows with several nods and a tired smile, and half-way out of the door she turned her head.

"We ... made him look, well, not too bad, before Professor Adachi let his wife go in for a minute or two to make her farewells. The fat man who was waiting outside here went off to be with her, I think. Is he a relative?"

"Not exactly, no. But he's the best person to comfort her at the moment. We shall take good care of Mrs. Migishima, Doctor."

Chapter 22

THE LAWYER SUSUMU NARITA BROKE BEFORE KOICHI Suminoe did, and I strongly suspect that much of the credit for that belongs to District Prosecutor Akamatsu. You'll recall that Akamatsu had told me earlier that he had come across Narita in the past and didn't trust him. It now seems to me quite possible that in fact Black Hole had for some time been putting together a dossier about him.

At all events he authorised, indeed urged us to arrest Narita on charges of conspiracy to murder; and by the time Hara and I began to interrogate him intensively the lawyer was ready to sing like a canary. We concluded that Akamatsu had almost certainly been in confidential touch with him and offered him some sort of deal provided he collaborated with us. I didn't ask, and Akamatsu didn't offer to enlighten me. In any case, by the time we'd finished our work the sentence Narita faced was likely to put him behind bars for most of his life even if Akamatsu asked for it to be reduced.

I should perhaps just explain at this point that although I left Hara nominally in charge of the investigation I made it clear to him that I expected to be actively involved in its closing stages, and in effect to be directing its handling.

Hara accepted the position with good grace and we worked together without any friction that I noticed.

For two or three days we left Koichi Suminoe to sweat, holding him on charges relating to comparatively minor offences against public order. Meantime we constructed a devastating case against him, on the basis of the evidence we already had and the additional information obtained from Narita.

When we eventually gave him the works, as Hara rather surprisingly expressed it, Suminoe crumbled completely. It took time and patience to get the full story out of him, but in the end he confessed to having been at the house that fatal Sunday and murdering his uncle. Then, almost by way of a casual afterthought, he admitted that he'd telephoned his brother Toshio on the morning of the second of January and asked him to meet him by the sculpture in the little park at a particular time to discuss something important. Intending to shoot him from Narita's office window and then "take care" of his uncle, as he put it. I thought I'd been convinced of that for some time, but it was surprisingly wounding to my self-esteem to have to accept once and for all that I'd simply been in the way that day.

The hoodlum who actually killed Migishima was simply a paid hit-man, the sort it's not too difficult to hire if you have the right connections. Noguchi was familiar with such characters and experienced in handling them, so we let him get on with it. Child's play, Ninja soon reported, having extracted the information that the gunman had been handed a million yen in cash by a man he'd never seen before to do the job, told where to show up and when, and been informed that someone would point out the target to him.

Ninja later mentioned in passing that the gunman expressed regret only over the fact that because he'd shot the wrong man he hadn't received the second million he'd been promised on completion. The prosecutor agreed that he'd press for the wretch to be put away for at least fifteen years.

The elder Suminoe had known, you see, that his brother

150

Toshio would be attending the union conference as a delegate. He'd also predicted, as any intelligent person could have done, that there would certainly be rightist demonstrations and very possibly disturbances outside the hall, under cover of which Toshio could be attacked. In spite of our having tried to leave him with a false sense of relative security, Narita must have warned him that we knew what was in the will. So he wasn't fool enough to have a second try at shooting Toshio himself.

I remain personally convinced that Suminoe's plan, reckless as it was anyway, would have depended for success on far too many imponderables unless he had, with his friend and fellow conspirator Narita, through his ultra-right contacts, somehow engineered the snake-dancing incident and the capture of Toshio's girl friend. It was her seizure that virtually guaranteed that Toshio would offer himself as a conspicuous target at a time of great confusion. Between them Narita and Suminoe had clearly been prepared to invest a good deal of money in order to lay their hands on a huge fortune later, and it certainly wouldn't have been beyond their capacity to have inserted an *agent provocateur* or two into the hall in the guise of delegates.

However that may be, there was no doubt that Koichi Suminoe had been standing directly beside the gunman when the shot was fired. Ninja Noguchi, who had been mingling with the crowd of bystanders, had spotted him earlier and moved in to keep an eye on him. You may recall that he'd earlier expressed some anxiety about Toshio Suminoe's safety. Alas, he hadn't reckoned on Suminoe's hiring somebody else to do his murderous work for him, and didn't see the gun in the thug's hand until it was too late.

Well, I expect you can piece together the remaining pieces of the puzzle for yourself. The much-vaunted "secret" will of the late Hideki Suminoe had been no secret from the moment he entrusted it to the care of his attorney Susumu Narita. We had forensic tests run on the envelope

151

in the possession of the District Prosecutor and they indicated that it had been opened and re-sealed at some point.

We have to deal in demonstrable facts and aren't paid to speculate after a case is closed. Nevertheless, it wouldn't surprise me to learn that Narita first violated the secrecy of the will out of nothing more than simple curiosity, nor that it was a long time before he first conceived the idea of putting himself into a position to benefit from its provisions personally.

As the pompous Hideki Suminoe's adviser over a long period Narita would, it seems to me, have been treated often enough to the old man's thoughts on life in general and his opinions of his two nephews in particular. It seems safe to theorise that he would have gathered that Toshio the dreamy idealist would never in a million years think of killing his cantankerous uncle, even if he had known that by doing so he could make himself rich. What would be the point, anyway? Toshio was young. He had only to wait for nature to take its course to inherit the lion's share of Hideki's money perfectly honourably.

His elder brother Koichi on the other hand stood to gain hugely, but only if Toshio were to die at more or less the same time as his uncle; that is, without the old man having the opportunity to revise his will before his own demise. I ask you, what sort of man could seriously consider embarking for profit on two murders that would have to be meticulously planned and timed? Answer, a greedy, clever, ingenious lawyer with a twisted mind, who thought he saw a way in which he could arrange for them to be committed by somebody else.

It's anybody's guess when Narita entered into his conspiracy with the elder nephew, but obvious that Koichi Suminoe was the man to approach. Perhaps Narita undertook a long and careful campaign to play on his weakness of character and his notorious financial irresponsibility.

He had material enough to employ in the process of poisoning Koichi's mind. Koichi must in any case have realised that his uncle Hideki didn't like him much, and

152

resented his closeness to Toshio. How, he might well have said to himself, had little, feeble Toshio managed to disregard his obligations to the family and the family company and yet somehow go on enjoying the run of his uncle's house? While he, Koichi, was not only a gifted computer expert able to make a real contribution to the business, but also diligent and interested?

You can see what I'm driving at. Even before he had any idea that the eccentric old Noh enthusiast had made only the most grudgingly conditional provision for him in his will, Koichi was almost certainly an embittered man. Hara and I wondered together quite often about the way Narita might have turned Koichi into his catspaw, and thought it likely that over a period he trapped him in a mesh of false friendship. By confessing confidentially to extreme right-wing sympathies on the safe assumption that a man keen on hunting and shooting probably shared them, for example, and lending him money to reduce his debts. Then, choosing the right psychological moment, revealing to Koichi the insulting truth about the will.

Do you have a better theory? If you do I'd be interested to hear it.

Chapter 23

As YOU'LL HAVE GATHERED, PUTTING TOGETHER THE CASES against Susumu Narita and Koichi Suminoe consumed a lot of time and energy, but heaven forbid that you should imagine that any of us took the death of Ken'ichi Migishima and the situation of his widow Junko lightly. On the contrary.

I like to think that we would have been deeply affected by the death in such a manner of any patrolman, even if he hadn't been based at headquarters and known so well as a person to most of us. As it was we were shattered by the loss of Migishima, and both Hara and I reproached ourselves for not having thought as carefully as we should have done about the possible consequences of releasing Toshio Suminoe from custody. Perhaps indeed that is why he and I buried ourselves in our work without squabbling over who was going to do what.

In the aftermath of the death we did all the conventional things expected of us, and I hope a few of the right ones also. You know of course that when a Japanese dies the usual thing is for a wake to be held at the home, and for a Buddhist priest to be invited to chant prayers and sutras there before the cremation takes place. There's also the business of condolence visits by neighbours, friends and colleagues of the deceased, who call to offer their respects and what we call "incense money" in special envelopes. The amount varies according to the status and means of the mourner, who usually knows or is advised what is expected of him or her, and the money is in most cases applied to the funeral expenses.

Migishima's parents were both still living, so these rituals took place at their house in the Nada ward on the eastern outskirts of Kobe, rather than in the small apartment on the other side of town that Junko and her husband had bought with the help of a huge mortgage loan. This might be the moment to mention that some months later, when Hideki Suminoe's will was at last probated, his principal heir Toshio persuaded Junko to let him pay off that mortgage by way of solatium and as an expression of his own grief over the way her husband had died tragically in protecting him.

It goes without saying that Toshio made a condolence visit to the house in Nada, and I'm pretty sure that every headquarters officer who ever had anything to do with Migishima put in an appearance there. Hanae accompanied me when I went, and though on such sad occasions nothing but the most formal words are spoken on either side, we were both greatly moved by the dignity of the comportment of Junko and of her parents-in-law.

One of the first things Kimura and I arranged—on the actual day of his death—was Migishima's formal promotion to senior patrolman. This was something I had the power to authorise myself. We fudged the effective date, too, so that in our personnel records he was shown as already holding that rank when killed on duty. This was no empty gesture: it made a significant difference to the amount of compensation and other benefits Junko would receive.

Furthermore, although it was not possible nor would it have been desirable in any case for me to break the news to her until several weeks later, as soon as Junko indicated

155

that after a period of compassionate leave she would wish to return to duty, I set in train the much more complicated process of getting her put on the National Police Agency strength as an assistant inspector.

I'm sorry to say that not many women police officers achieve what you might call commissioned rank, but I'd long considered that Junko had the ability, style and potential to rise high if she stayed in the service. I had to twist a good many arms to get this proposal approved, but I succeeded in the end, with a useful boost in the form of strong official support from Prosecutor Akamatsu. In fact Black Hole, who had for so long been the bane of my existence, became in my last months of service a reliable ally and even, though I don't want to overstate the case, a kind of friend.

A few days after the private family funeral ceremonies we held a formal memorial gathering to honour the late Senior Patrolman Ken'ichi Migishima, at the public hall outside which he had died the previous week. I insisted that every stop should be pulled out for the occasion, and got the chairman of the prefectural public safety commission to loosen the purse-strings he controlled, in order to ensure that no expense was spared. No amount of ceremony could do poor Migishima any good, I know, but I believe it offered some solace to his widow and his parents.

The hall is designed to accommodate about five hundred people. It was packed, and by no means exclusively with relatives, police officers and officials. The stage was banked with white and yellow flowers—don't ask me what kind they were—surrounding the centrepiece, a huge framed enlargement of a photograph of Migishima, looking so young and proud in his uniform that it nearly broke my heart to see it. The regional police brass band was in attendance, and played solemn music as people took their seats.

Migishima's father and mother were in places of honour in the front row, and Junko sat near them, with Ninja

156

Noguchi at her side as before. He was the only one of our headquarters team not in uniform—which would in any case have looked utterly absurd and incongruous on him—but looked most dignified in a good dark suit and white shirt with black tie and black armband.

I'd been advised in advance that Junko had asked that Kimura should be allotted the seat on her other side, and was pleased so see that from time to time he touched her hand briefly and discreetly in support and reassurance. Who knows, when the pain of bereavement has diminished to some degree, the two of them might be drawn to each other. Although he doesn't like admitting it, Kimura's getting a bit old for the role of playboy, and Junko should certainly not face a virtual lifetime of lonely widowhood.

Hara and Kimura each wore their Number Ones, while I had on—for the very last time—my full ceremonial dress uniform as Director General of the force. The governor of the prefecture, the mayor of Kobe, the chairman of the public safety commission and District Prosecutor Akamatsu were in morning dress, as were the more senior of the other civilian officials present. There was no particular reason why the president of the teachers' union should have felt any obligation to attend, but he did, and it was good of him. He made a point of approaching and speaking to Junko afterwards, I noticed. So did Toshio Suminoe.

You want to know about the speeches? I wouldn't dream of boring you with them, especially as my own was supposed to be the most important one. All I'll tell you is that whether or not Junko and her parents-in-law were in any state of mind to take in what I said, I'd given a lot of care and thought to preparing my remarks, and discussed my draft with Hanae. I got through it without mishap, and like to think that I did honour to a fine young officer.

Having visited the Migishima house to pay her respects, Hanae had, with my full agreement, decided against going to the memorial meeting as well. She never did have much taste for exchanging meaningless clichés with officials on

157

formal occasions, and knew I'd have to dance attendance on the local VIPs before and after the ceremony. At least I was paid to do it, but it was an emotionally draining afternoon, and after changing out of my black finery with the silver insignia in the privacy of my office and back into my workaday civilian suit I was glad to be driven home.

Unfortunately, however, I didn't arrive back to the atmosphere of peace and sympathetic understanding I'd been looking forward to. In fact there was no answer to my routine "I'm home" shout as I entered the house. I did, however, hear odd sniffing sounds coming from upstairs, so in my stockinged feet I went to investigate.

In the big room where we sleep and which doubles as a reception room on the rare occasions we have company, I found Hanae, gently patting the back of a sobbing Michiko. Hanae was facing the open doorway, and as soon as she caught my eye she made a complicated but extremely eloquent little movement with her free hand. It said, "Nothing personal, but leave us alone for a while, would you?"

So I went quietly downstairs, put my shoes and coat on again and pottered down to a little bar I know near Rokko Station. There I treated myself to a couple of glasses of the Scotch and water I often turn to in the aftermath of a crisis, and gazed glumly at some silly quiz programme being shown on the TV set mounted above the bar. Just my luck: there was one of those awful grinning Japanese-speaking *gaitare* Westerners on the panel.

When I thought I'd wasted enough time, I walked up the hill again and reached home to find, as I'd hoped, that Michiko had left. Hanae then told me what I'd already guessed, namely that Hara had told Michiko he wanted to break off their affair.

She'll get over it, I suppose, but you know, Mr. Melville, I often wonder if Hara really made the right decision.